Love Is A Solitary Runner...

- A NOVEL -

ARVIND JOSHI

INDIA • SINGAPORE • MALAYSIA

ISBN

Hardcase 979-8-89446-820-4
Paperback 979-8-89415-324-7

Chapter One

I was born into a conservative Hindu family where naming a newborn too had to align with the stars shining nonchalantly millions of miles away. My father affectionately named me "SARA" meaning "precious" in my native tongue, Hindi. When he took me in his arms for the very first time, with glinted eyes, he emphatically said to my mother, "She is the most precious gift that you and this life have ever bestowed upon me."

If inheritance is the prerogative of every child, then I am firm in believing that I inherited my father's rebellious spirit and my mother's tenacity, ready to take on the world. Yet, it was to the dismay of the family's orthodox approach contemplating anxiously upon my fate, reminiscing about how it could not dissuade my father from cherishing the lifelong dream of serving in the Indian Army as a PARA COMMANDO officer, one of the most lethal sections of the Indian Army. If only it were possible to shield a girl's heart from the truth in her grandparents' eyes: maybe I could have too, ignored the smouldering apprehension in their eyes of losing me too, like their son, to the insatiable urge of pursuing one's dreams rather than acquiescing to unremitting dogma.

My admission to a co-ed school, by my father's consent, at the tender age of four, rendered possibly the most indelible memory of that time through my deeply conservative grandparents. It was a sheer frenzy in the house when Grandpa first saw me in the Army School uniform. I was cocooned in Mom's lap and could see Grandpa, usually an indolent one, jerking his whole posture with one hand gesticulating rhythmically at Papa, while Grandma was gawking impassively upon me. Mother pressed me tenaciously to her bosom. I could feel her heart pounding faster than usual and sensed a faint lump of whimper in her arid throat caged by her self-confined will.

Much to the relief of my grandparents, the Army School, where I began my formal education, maintained a strict yet conducive environment for education and overall development. I always felt a strange harmony in aligning my purposeless childhood tantrums with the meticulous yet equally affectionate teachers of that esteemed institution. I still recall a foggy morning in wintry January when our class was to be relocated. The benches, still lying outside, were yet to be arranged. Sawdust covered the floor, likely remnants from recent woodwork. As we stepped inside, to our surprise, it resembled a skating rink, with our feet barely gripping the floor. Soon, every student was enjoying skidding and making loud, hooting noises, their bodies floating aimlessly as if in the ether of their own imagination.

Tired of this unexpected adventure, I rested against the windowpane.

Through the frosted glass, I glimpsed a faint image of our class teacher Mrs. Raman, observing us meditatively from outside, braving the chilling fog. She wrapped herself tenderly in a gracious blue Pashmina shawl, her hands tightly gripping our attendance register. I felt a strange, confident solace in her selfless demeanour.

I adored seeing my father in the uniform, especially when he used to scrutinise himself discreetly in front of the mirror, much to the envy of any beautiful woman in the prime of her youth.

"Bhow!" I used to exclaim, pulling him out of his trance-like state. Each time, he pretended to shudder at my tantrums as if he too loved seeking refuge in my innocent little world, as I loved seeking refuge in his too arduous one for me to comprehend. When I matured enough to discern beyond our blissful interactions, I dared to unravel the insignia of the Parachute Regiment, scrubbing with my novice hands and gazing at it meditatively. He then removed his cap and explained, "Partially behind the circle with the Parachute Regiment insignia there's an open parachute, with wings spread out from the circle. You can also see a dagger superimposed on the parachute and the upper portion of the circle-" I watched his fingers move with firm commands, though his voice didn't quiver once during the entire description of the insignia. He then put on his maroon beret bearing the insignia and marched off in silence, leaving me fumbling with inhibitions and unspoken words. Nervously I looked for him and there he was with an ambushing, unfathomable gaze as if acknowledging my audacity with a gentle smile.

The annual day celebrations in our school were always eagerly awaited by students and teachers alike; it was a chance to prove one's mettle to fellow students, teachers, and parents. Incidentally, it was my tenth birthday on the same day and Papa had planned a bash at home after the event celebrations. As part of the curriculum, there were events organised exclusively for parents to participate in. Dad excelled in the sack race and bicycle balancing while, Mom surprised us all by exhibiting great dexterity and winning the eagerly watched "Musical-Chair" competition. I had my own plans too; it was my birthday after all and I wanted to make it special, etched forever in the memories of the hero of my life, my beloved father.

The last segment of the day was probably the most jam-packed as well. It was designed exclusively for children and involved their candid expressions for their parents through any possible means. "Let the child's mind fly," said Mrs. Raman, formally commencing the final act of the day. I could hear the clamour from backstage, fueling my nervousness with every passing second, thoughts like, "What if I can't do it? What if I fumbled with the words?" were consuming me. I felt all the butterflies of the world tickling me to exhaustion and amid this turmoil they finally announced my name on stage. Walking those precise ten steps from where I stood in the dark to the stage curtain felt like the most burdensome steps tread in my benign little life.

My heart shuddered as they raised the curtain and fixed the spotlight on me. I saw parents sitting in the second row. My father coughed tenderly. I looked into his eyes, and with trembling hands, I dared to lift his maroon beret and spoke in a monotone, "Partially behind the circle with the Parachute Regiment insignia is an open parachute. Wings are spread out from the circle. You can also see a dagger superimposed on the parachute and the upper portion of the circle." Every gaze seemed frozen upon me. I was shaking when the beret was finally dropped from my trembling hands, which were still not steady enough to hold it firmly. Then, I saw him leaping towards the stage. My saviour, my hero. I pressed my face against his thumping heart and wept relentlessly while there was thunderous applause in the background.

Chapter Two

It was a dark, windy night of December and the valley of Srinagar was struck by a relentless storm. I saw a shadow mumbling impatiently in the darkness from the study. I was about to scream when a severe thunderbolt in the night sky splashed father with its white light followed by an objectionable grunt. His gaze was fixed upon the "Ashok Chakra" which was recently conferred to him for successfully thwarting a major terrorist insurgency in the valley. I could see a thousand unvented emotions trapped in his frozen vivid eyes as he stood stoically in the dark.

Five years had passed since we left Ambala Cantt and shifted to Srinagar. It was the year 1999 and the country was on the brink of another war with an uneasy neighbour. I was appearing for my matriculation standard in the same year and was studying in the Army School over there. Albeit in strenuous times like these, Papa never let his war concerns and other duties afflict my studies. He was meticulous in Mathematics and throughout my studies up to that time, I never opted to study in any private coaching institutes for this nightmarish subject. I rather enjoyed it too much in his guidance and always topped it, much to the envy of my fellow students and the instigation of an ethereal, harmless pride in me.

When the examinations were finally over, Mother and I were off to the maternal grandparents' home in New Delhi. It was a compulsory harsh decision that we had to endure for there was a threat of an imminent war looming upon the nation. Grandpa was a retired civil servant and Grandma was a humble homemaker. I observed him to be very punctilious in his manners and I often snubbed him for being too boorish and snobbish of a person. But I had to know deeply about what exactly was going on in the war and with my limited abilities to understand the world around; it was certainly indispensable on my part to form a sort of obligatory acquaintance with him. Hence I started with being too modest and servile to his methodological ways of living. I often used to see him brooding over the poetry of Tagore and the other eminent western writers. Luckily, we studied Coleridge's *The Rhyme of the Ancient Mariner* in our English literature curriculum for matriculation and it was my seemingly possible connection to his otherwise phlegmatic mind.

So, I finally decided to insinuate myself into his arid and impervious world with Mariner on my side! I was yet anticipating the right moment to take my chance upon this tricky and foolhardy voyage until one day, I finally interrupted him from his trance-like state while he was too engrossed with the works of Wordsworth. "Nana, we too read *The Rhyme of the Ancient Mariner* this year in our literature section." He winced as if my audacity was merely an odious effort connoting barging in of a contemptible novice into the mind of the intelligentsia. He fixed his hawk-like cruel stare upon me and replied in a contemptuous tone.

"When Samuel Taylor Coleridge wrote this marvellous poem, it was truly and widely known and rightly acclaimed as *The Rime of Ancyent Marinere* and that was how Mr. Coleridge might have written it and would have desired too for the world to remember. I must say, we call this world a civilised and developed one, when we don't revere the authenticity of achievements." When he crooned *The Rime of Ancyent Marinere* I felt a pang of mockery inside my heart as if all of this was intended to demean me and my lousy existence in his eyes. With all my courage and dignity, I could not muster the strength to face him for one moment more. I flounced out of the room and slammed the door with obtrusive intentions.

After that, I was certain that I'd never be able to breach inside the mind of this prima donna, until one day he ended his implacable hostility himself. "So what did you learn from Coleridge's masterpiece?" I was bewildered and almost felt taken by surprise, yet I was firm on my purpose to learn as much as I could about the war, and he was probably the only one there to instil me with the right information.

"This masterpiece of Coleridge is definitely an archetype of poetry. I have never encountered myself with any work of poetry so rhythmically poised between motive and realm of uncertainties. His majestic work has the power to grip one's mind and not leave it from the outset till the end."

"Very accurate I must say! But I believe you might not have read the whole of it. I have seen that in your curriculum they have ended it at the time when the fellow sailors hang the Albatross about the Mariner's neck." I nodded in affirmation to which he continued further.

"Hmmm... The poem doesn't actually end here. Mr. Coleridge takes us to much turbulent storms after that." He lighted his cigar and puffed twice. I could see the smoke levitating, inundating his already murkier demeanour. He stood looming upon me, exploring my eyes and mind in an uncomfortable, smothering silence. Hesitatingly, I spoke abruptly…

"I would like to see how and where these rough seas end!" He turned around and plodded towards the door with smoke still hovering around as if personifying a clinging, stalwart ally.

"Tomorrow, we will start from where you were left off." With these final words for the day, he left my room. My apparent intentions at the moment of slamming the door upon his face yet his decision to think beyond my dissent and be acquiesced to my insinuation raised certain queries in my mind. But for now, I was immersed with a feeling of triumph and very much wanted to enjoy this girlish propensity.

Grandpa was a wonderful tutor. I could not believe that in the motif of such a rigid character, there lay obscured a passionate scholar, whose heart throbbed like that of a young lover, for the coveted beauty of literature. My perception towards literature metamorphosed through his emphatic understanding and equally brilliant deliverance of the hidden nuances of the beautiful subject. I was not ashamed to say this but never before had I enjoyed reading the *Marinere* as much as I did it with him explaining it to me during our long walks in the evening.

As I became more acquainted with him, I learned that it was very obvious for him to despise the ordinary. In fact, while exacting upon his standards of perception, I developed a certain sympathy for him; for he was not despising the ordinary but was an admirer and a sort of saviour of simplicity in the guise of condescension; vehemently concealing his own identity for being too vulnerable in one's path to be neglected. But strangely, he was not scared of being neglected as much as he was anxious about being unable to find one apt heir for this onerous path which had sort of become a raison d'etre for his impervious existence. With every passing day, I could see the ascending expectations in his eyes for me, yet for me, the burden was too aghast to bear.

Feared of meandering off my original purpose and profaning his hopes for me, one day I boldly asked him, "Nana, how did this war begin and when will it supposedly end?" He smiled and took me in his lap and spoke in a tender voice. "Your father called up yesterday. I wished to wake you up but he insisted not to disturb you in your sleep. Everything's fine over there and speculations are that there will be a ceasefire very shortly. All efforts are channelised for peace."

I could not believe he deduced my intentions so deftly. I felt an instant urge to abandon all my astuteness to his wisdom.

An uncontrollable tear fell upon his toe while my head reposed comfortably upon his knee. He caressed gently and spoke in his conventionally commanding tone.

"Due to extreme cold conditions in the winters, as a pact of mutual agreement and understanding between both the nations' armies, it was a common practice to abandon some forward posts on their respective sides of LOC (Line of Control), which actually is a military control line between the two nations. On their side is the former part of the state of Jammu and Kashmir. Not until the month of May this year, some local shepherds reported sighting enemy intrusions in Kargil. In response to that, our army sent up a patrolling party, the members of which were captured and then tortured to death. As the days progressed, there were reports of enemy shelling in Kargil with first infiltration sightings in adjoining Dras, Kaksar and Mushkoh districts. By mid-May, the army mobilised more troops to the Kargil sector and with the start of June, what was earlier perceived as an incursion morphed into mankind's worst necessary facet, a War!"

He was silent, as if contemplating his stance, while this worst facet stared deeply into his keen yet weary eyes. I held his hand and tried to console him, striving to deny his speculation that, like all the others who crossed his life, I too would abandon him forlorn, much like his own fate, in his chosen, arduous self-inflictions.

Chapter Three

It was already mid-June, and the war had gruesomely lunged into its second month. Never before had the media been so close in covering the entire operation as it was now. Our whole family used to remain glued to the TV set for the latest updates of the war, while brave media reporters endured the war to let the common man know the progress and to make him and the nation realise how a handful of strangers, abandoning almost everything, risking their lives, got ready to face the fusillade on the call of duty. One of those strangers altruistically facing the fusillade was my father, and this burgeoning thought was enough to torment me silently, as for hours I brooded over the callously lopsided world we were living in.

My matriculation result was declared in the same month, and I was the topper of the class with a ninety-four percent aggregate. It pleased me even more that I topped in Mathematics in the entire region. All of this invoked those beautiful moments I spent with my father to master the intricate yet equally beautiful subject. It was a welcome reason to celebrate for the family. But, of course, everyone had scruples about enjoying the occasion until finally Grandpa took the initiative and planned to laud my achievement by arranging a small get-together party at home. Our guest list was not so long as my friends were scattered now. The people invited were from the very elite social class, for they were Grandpa's circle of acquaintances. It was my first brush-up with the sophistication of society, and honestly, I felt a bit vulnerable towards it.

I could see the slim and svelte ladies garrulously boasting with a hint of envy frozen vividly in their eyes, as if divulging the very farcical camaraderie they pretended to cherish as a symbol of their class. I wasn't too sure about what notions they kept for me behind their beaming faces, yet I was a bit concerned too about it. Grandpa sensed the same and spoke gently to me. "Dear, it's true that blood is thicker than water, but thicker than blood nowadays is the obligation of sustaining the symbiosis of society. Despite all the ugliness you might be seeing around, you'd one day realise that it has now become an indispensable aspect of society which ironically contributes to the happiness among people through its own peculiar ways."

Probably I was still too young to decipher those social whirligigs and those necessary sacrifices made by people for the sake of a so-called meaningful existence. But I was content with my vulnerability, for it acted like a shield in favour of my will to not mingle among the people I felt uncomfortable to be with, despite obligations demanding the absolute opposite from me.

My confrontation with something never experienced before forced me to introspect on certain facets of human nature, and suddenly I felt a strong urge to explore the city whose history was very much alike my own ravenous impetus, for it never let any single authority consistently rule over it for a reasonable period of time.

One fine Sunday, I finally managed to convince Nana to plan a complete day-long tour of the historical city. We visited certain great monuments like India Gate, Qutub Minar, Red Fort, Old Fort, Humayun's Tomb, and it consumed the majority of our days' time until finally, we decided to end our tour in the serene labyrinths of another mystical monument called "Jantar-Mantar". While I was trying to frame the purpose of the individual structures of the place, Nana seemed lost in translation, as if trying to delve into his own soul trapped somewhere in the stories of the historic city, until his words finally managed to seek refuge from the clutches of a very engrossing past of an equally captivating city.

"You know, first there were Ghulams who ruled the city from 1206-1290 AD, and then there were Khilgis from 1290-1320 AD. Then there were Tughlaqs, Sayyids, and Lodis, who ruled the city until 1526 AD. From 1526 AD onwards, the city inherited the leadership of Mughals until they too were overpowered and ultimately dethroned by the British, who ruled for almost two hundred years and then finally were ousted in the year 1947. This whole bloody struggle is engraved upon the soul of this city, which sometimes makes me wonder whether this city is like an infidel mistress or if it had always been cursed to be ruled over by incapable masters."

By the beginning of July, the war had tantalisingly maneuvered into a favourable position for the nation. In the very first week, the Army launched a three-pronged attack in Kargil. One of the most historic events of the entire war was the recapture of the "Point 5353", famously known as the "Tiger Hill." Nana narrated to me the entire tale of the magnificent valour many times, and it never failed to infuse a refulgent courage in my passionate heart.

Papa's clandestine operations in the Kargil war could never be known to us through any media coverage, albeit the nine Para (SF) had taken a strategic part in the follow-up raids and reconnaissance operations, one of the most enduring and risky missions of any army in the war. I was too thrilled to know the tales of bravery of my father's elite 9 Para (SF) from Nana, as he told me that due to the active involvement of the unit in the "Batalik Sector", it was conferred with the Bravest of the Brave citation.

On the fateful day of July 26, 1999, the Kargil conflict finally came to an end as the Indian Army firmly declared the complete eviction of the intruders. It was Diwali-like celebrations in the whole nation, and there was no exception at our place too. Mama and Grandma illuminated the entire home with earthen lamps. The special delicacies made for the day, smeared with their love and perfection, only corroborated the resolute will of the family to not let things fall apart even if the adversity is as catastrophic as the war itself.

It was early Sunday morning, and at precisely seven in the morning, the telephone started ringing relentlessly. It was Nana who first attended the call, and within moments of his receiving the call, he was bellowing, to our surprise! His befuddled voice made us wonder what possibly could impair his otherwise commanding, confident accent. It was me who first reached for his call in somnolence. I could see his quivering face failing to utter the words from his somewhat parched throat until I bent forward to listen to his choked voice. I heard him saying, "Your Papa is on the line." My heart ached as I heard him calling, "Sara, Sara! Darling, are you there?" The receiver appeared to be frozen in the numb hands of Nana, who, like me, from the piety of all of my life's sanity put together, could not muster the courage to acknowledge him with his ordeals while we were cocooned in our lives thousands of miles away. At last, my heart revolted against the patience, and I took the call. "Papa, how are you? I terribly miss you, we all do Papa! Please come home soon!" My mind was too dumbfounded to make sense of the situation, and he knew it, and like always, he came to my rescue even when he was hundreds of miles away.

"Sara! Congrats on your brilliant result, dear. I am so proud of you for your remarkable achievement, and more than that, I am glad that you held the family together in the face of crisis. Your Nana told me everything, and I am so happy for all your efforts. It gives immense warmth to my soul here in the frozen, barren lands."

Our conversation lasted for almost an hour, and I came to know that he'd have to be posted there for some time more until there are no further incidents of serious incursions reporting again from the enemy side. Meanwhile, I shared everything with him too, be it my silly inhibitions on the sophistications of society, my initial ordeal with Nana, or my exploration of the historic city with him, and like always, he was an impeccable listener to all of my silly blabs. Although I knew that every word was precious to him and he'd be engraving them elegantly in the robust canvas of his heart, I also knew that embedded along the solace of my words there'd be the frigid, impassive pain which he'd never let me inherit. Sometimes during the conversation, my eyes met with Nana's; and every time there was the same agonising concern, "For how could we be worthy of his salutations?"

My father died in the same year while thwarting a major terrorist insurgency merely three months after the Kargil war. His funeral was arranged with full military honours. So many people had so much to say about him, yet the words of one of his seniors affected me the most.

"Major SabyaSachi Vasishta, aka 'The Hawk', his revered name among his men, is an unbearable loss to our elite 9

Para family. His unflinching valour glints in the eyes of those who saw his gallantry at the time when he was unfettered by the volley of shots fired to arrest his movement; yet it could not incarcerate the courage of his heart. He killed four terrorists and guided his fellow men to the successful accomplishment of the mission. In the whole operation, a lot many lives could have been lost, but it was Major Vasishta's impeccable bravery and sacrifices which not only averted the further tragedy but also evacuated the terrorists. The Army nominates his name for the 'Param Veer Chakra', the highest Gallantry award to her brave sons."

They shot twenty-one guns in honour of my father, lying serene on the funeral pyre with his body wrapped in the National Flag, which was soon going to be our most cherished inheritance. We were allowed to see him for the last time. I saw Nana and Grandpa offering condolences to one another, I saw his fellow men saluting him one by one, and then finally I saw Mother, who bent forward towards his face while her lips parted slightly; I knew those were her last words to him. Finally, it was my turn, and I advanced slightly towards his pyre. I was recalling the annual day where I described the insignia of the Para Regiment. I saw his same Maroon Beret swaddled closely to him amid all the farewell messages and flowers. As they lit the pyre, I had the Beret with me. It was something bequeathed by destiny to me as a modicum of an undecipherable yet priceless inheritance.

Mama and I decided to spend the rest of our time left with Nana in New Delhi. Immediately after Papa's death,

Mama was offered an administrative job in the "Army Wives Welfare Association" (AWWA), to which she accepted gracefully. AWWA was a voluntary organisation of the Indian Army that served for the well-being of Army Wives and Children and was dedicated to the rehabilitation of war widows and differently abled.

It was the twilight of July, and the Delhi skyline was overcast with thick, malevolent Nimbus. I was sitting on the veranda when I saw Nana come and sit beside me.

"Nana, when the Mariner killed the Albatross, he suffered in destitute. I remember his words…

'I look'd to Heaven and tried to pray;

But ere a prayer had gusht,

A wicked whisper came and made

My heart as dry as dust.'

Is Heaven so callous to our prayers?" Nana held my hand and took me to the garden while it was drizzling. He looked meditatively and cited the lines of Coleridge's immortal.

"O sleep, it is a gentle thing.

Beloved from pole to pole!

To Mary-queen the praise be given;

She sent the gentle sleep from Heaven

That slid into my soul."

"Your father has been bestowed with the sleep of a martyr by the heavens. A martyr sleeps with no rage or resentment left in his heart, even for his enemies."

The Nimbus showered all they could upon us. Never before had I felt so gratifying drenched in the rain. The words of Nana reverberated in my soul, and the music of clouds and rain seemed as an elegy for the martyrs sung solemnly from Heaven.

Chapter Four

I could never study mathematics thenceforth. This enervating inhibition towards the great subject ensued on account of the irrevocable loss, when the numbers to me were nothing more than a hysterical, nauseating nostalgia now. Papa once said, 'Sara, the great Galileo had once said that mathematics is the language with which the God wrote the Universe, so if you want to decipher the world around; learn to decipher mathematics.'

It might have been the language with which the God wrote the Universe, yet it could not quench my inane inhibitions which could merely have been a corollary of a much complex equation pertaining to a similarly complex motif. This could be interestingly apt for the serenity of a conditioned mind; but my mind was not conditioned and neither had I wanted it to be. I chose my path to struggle and seek the reasons of the baffling lopsidedness of the world, to explore the truth of a morality which motivates the actions of people ultimately leading to the irrevocable changes in the lives of millions.

I wanted to enquire in the eyes of piety, for how could it ruin peace for the sake of an unknown higher one? With notions like these, mathematics was too aloof a possibility for the strenuous path that coerced into a mean dissection of human soul. So I chose psychology for the rest of my life, for it was adept and could fortify me against the unseen, unprecedented war which was now an inseparable part of my life.

Nana's painstaking efforts in carving the path for my chosen field of study led me finally to the doors of Carmel College of Psychology, one of the most coveted and prestigious institutes for pursuing psychology in the whole nation. The undergraduate course at the premier institute extensively covered all the important subfields of psychology like social, cultural, cognitive, counselling, clinical, organisational, lifespan, and biopsychology to name a few.

Our curriculum was meticulously planned. It comprehensively covered practical exercises, analysis, group discussions, role plays and my personal favourite 'Field Trips', for it tested our skills and knowledge to its limits through implementing them on strangers and not familiar faces.

One of the most arduous yet equally engrossing projects of psychology was to derive a complete psycho-analysis of any random person preferably coded as a 'Subject'. Due to my defense background, I never faced any serious problem while interacting or being acquainted with strangers or foreign places. Incidentally, I was always the most thorough and accurate in envisaging the real person camouflaged amid the strata of self-willed deception of character, acting like a safeguard for vulnerability or prowess of cognition for propitious survival.

With time, I developed an impressive reputation in the institute through my consistent performance in academics as well as practical or field performances. This caught the attention of our Head of Department, Dr. Vinita Sikand, who was also our lecturer for Cognitive Psychology. One fine day I was summoned to her office after our academic hours.

As I entered her office, I saw a frame hanging upon the wall with a handwritten quote of 'Gautam Buddha' inside it. It read *"No one saves us but ourselves, No one can and no one may. We ourselves must walk the path."* The whole aspect of a hanging frame with deftly executed strokes of her own handwriting was enough for me to surmise that her life could not be encompassed in the realms of one psychology but many.

We exchanged passing glances while she gestured for me to have a seat. While meditatively perceiving upon the frame, she finally broke the uncomfortable silence and asked me in a very nonchalant manner, "Do you know until the 1870s, the subject of Psychology was a branch of Philosophy?"

"Ah, yes indeed, Madam. Although the behavioural and other mind-related studies have been traced back to the history of ancient Greeks, yet it wasn't until the 1870s that the Germans and Americans developed it as an independent scientific discipline."

"Personally, I've been a big fan of philosophy and I firmly believe that so diverse and covert a subject like psychology could only be the inception of philosophy, the only subject that dares to unravel the purpose of the whole existence. So tell me Sara, what notions you keep for the vicious, cacophonic wars inside the seemingly serene mind of a philosopher; which often end upon their graves only."

Her hands levitated as if seeking their peace, making it altogether too dramatic for me to comprehend the real purpose of the summon. However, I was too sure upon the fact that this dross-looking event stored inside some far-fetched prospects.

"In fact, Madam, I never followed the works of any philosopher too seriously. With due respect, I revere their sacrifices for the relentless chase of truth, yet I believe that it's not philosophers alone but a simple layman can comprehend the nuances of philosophy as deftly as them; the difference being only in the kernel shrouded in the intricacies of philosophical jargon that emanates from a scholar's mouth while the same truth can be seen in the eyes of a layman burdened under the compulsion of survival. The world is often prejudiced over pretentious."

"But isn't the survival of our layman directly or indirectly dependent upon this society itself? So tell me Sara, isn't this kernel motivated by the interests of society? Then how can you compare the truth of a layman to the truth of a philosopher who never gets motivated by these interests but with the truth alone?"

"Very true, but the interests of society can never be extricated from the truth of a philosopher. Had it been so, the wars waged inside their minds could not have been that bloody and cacophonous. Philosophers toil hard to mend the very course of society to an ideal state, which is also the dream of a layman, for he yearns for it more desperately than them; as in the end it's him who actually gets affected the most in this perpetual tussle between ideal and erroneous one!"

"Then what are his contributions and efforts against the erroneous one? History is proof that every great revolution against tyranny was the inception of an enlightened mind. How can dreaming alone for that blissful, ideal state suffice the injustice tolerated by your layman or I must say can the survival suffice the cost of enduring a morally corrupt society?"

"Madam, a philosopher's relentless urge to unravel the nature and its laws and in the end to forge a path to a moral society is indeed very similar to the layman's quest for survival.

Both these aspects are actually two poles of a rational existence of a civil code, and along the axis of these aspects, rotates our lives. An ideal society, for its own peaceful existence, needs both." I was silent for a while until the stoic heart finally took over my aching mind as a bulwark against the soul's vulnerability.

"My father was one of those laymen who knew very well the power of Nature and the vulnerable human situation. He knew that nothing in this world is perfect yet he ended his life for the worst of human follies, better known as the War. Yes it's true that he sacrificed his life for this Nation but aren't these bloody wars merely envisaging our meaningless existence for the sake of the continuum of events? Yet we take part, we walk, we strive, not for the sake of being marionettes of the continuum but to acknowledge ourselves as part of one grand plan, where there are no biases or prejudices but a blissful equanimity.

No matter how hard I tried, it was impossible to shield myself from experiencing the turbulence of an emotional jolt pertaining to the traumatic past mishaps which I endured. I knew she somehow sensed it in my eyes until finally she said, 'Your Nana is my very good friend Sara! When you were admitted to this elite institute, he took my promise in helping you out in every possible manner. All this discussion was to analyse your bend of mind so that I could help you in making certain correct decisions regarding your career and overall life. But before I proffer you something, it's important for me to know what you have decided for your future after the completion of this Psychology Honours."

This startling revelation struck me. I tried to infer that it might be her clever tricks of psychology to have a fine dig of my mind for the sake of her own compulsive persuasions; I tested her by dragging her back to our incomplete conversation.

"Are my plans more important than this debate, Madam?" She adjusted the frame upon the wall once again and with a cursory glance towards me, she said.

"The fate of a layman has slipped numerous times while striving for the balance between survival and the elusive truth. But more obtrusively, the survival factor always faded out the truth callously from their lives. Yet I feel happy for you as you keep the pity and courage for them in times like these. But I warn you of this treacherous path. A lot many pious lives have been lost in these maelstroms of ever-changing ethics and moral codes."

"A chance to make the difference is everyone's privilege I suppose." "But of course! Then why not take it seriously? Full time maybe! How about a Sabbatical?"

"What kind of sabbatical leads to a platform like such?"

"When I was in the final year of my PhD in cognitive, there was a stoic, reticent fellow in our batch. He was one hell of an observant yet apt only for penning down his observations. He could never heal people albeit no one could feel the trauma and pain of others as astutely as him. Our HOD advised him a sabbatical for learning to open him up. When he returned, he was toned, precise and absolute."

"Yet I fear there might be a sabbatical for my vision."

Her gaze was fixed upon two students practicing with their respective subjects in the lush green lawn until she turned to me abruptly and said.

"Never think yourself too alone or too crowded in this world. It never fails to disappoint you and your beliefs. Tomorrow at sharp five in the evening, I'll come to your place for I want to introduce you to someone. You have almost a day's time to make the final choice."

Chapter Five

"It could never be an easy decision to choose the sabbatical over the plans of pursuing further education for anyone, and that too when all the relevant conditions are favourable for you to go for the higher studies and you have immense faith in your abilities to carve out the path to your goals. I discussed the possible course of action for my future with Nana, and he suggested I follow Mrs. Sikand's advice, which was quite expected of him too.

That same night, I contemplated hard over the sabbatical thing, which seemed as if offered to derail my meticulous ways of doing things! I tried to figure out numerous permutations for any possible propitious outcome; even juxtaposed the entire programme with respect to my interests, yet to my dismay, I could hardly conceive any plausible reason to continue with it, which only fueled the unwelcome anxiety and dilemma. However, there lay a silver lining to the whole scenario since there definitely could be more chances to encounter twisted situations and meet new people, which altogether served as a brilliant learning opportunity.

On the day of our last exam of the final semester, we were too excited to embark upon the future as no longer 'Novices' of a bygone time. Yet I felt more or less the same for obtrusive reasons.

As per the plan, I met Madam Sikand at sharp five in the evening. She took me along to her place and on our way, I came to know that we'd be heading to attend a piano concert at Wayne's auditorium. The occasion was the International Arts Festival in the city. I had never been to a piano performance before and neither did I know too much of the flair pertaining to the same, which only vacillated my mood further, yet I was left with no choice but to see where the rabbit hole ended.

As we made there, certain foreign artists were performing pieces of classical artists like Beethoven, Mozart, and Chopin. Madam herself was very fond of Western classical music and in that serene ambience of the auditorium, I too felt elated and sort of relieved myself in those symphonies and sonatas. It was as if the music pierced through me and strived to alleviate the unseen wounds of my heart. My trance-like state was unwillingly disturbed by the sweet yet commanding voice of the female orator.

"And now, ladies and gentlemen, we present to you Rachmaninoff's famous 'Piano Concerto No. 2' in C minor." For another few minutes, she named the artists of the orchestra until finally, she announced the pianist. I was quite surprised to hear an Indian name for the pianist.

My curiosity was, however, pacified by the tranquility of that brilliant piece of music. I closed my eyes amid the live performance and framed the story of my life so far. I felt my mind and heart setting loose of the obdurate demeanour. I could feel them settling into the coziness of their favourite memories. I did not feel like pulling them back, for I refused to play the usual role of a strict martinet at that very moment.

Amid the stream of an untamed consciousness of my life, I could feel my heart and mind being ensconced to the shores of their esteemed times, and myself sailing vulnerable, amok. With glinted eyes, I saw the impassive face of the pianist, as if he, through the power of the music alone, could redeem me; set me free of all my pains. I saw him wincing several times with his eyes closed, as if he too was aware of my pain and could feel it too. I hopelessly felt like both of us were en route to the same destination.

Once again, I closed my eyes and this time I didn't complain when the tears failed to sway their precious ones. The sudden applause from the enthralled audience with an occasional "Bravo, Bravo, Encore!" brought me back to the realms of reality. In the spotlight, I saw a certain inconceivable expression upon the pianist's face. He seemed to me a man of noble mien; although in those guised twitches of his expressions, I sensed an enigmatic, kind of hermetic existence within, which I wished not to stir at all. I was about to speak a few words in praise of the pianist to Madam when she said...

"His name is Siddhartha Pathak. Of course, a brilliant pianist yet not a professional. By profession, he is a successful consulting psychologist. An eminent social figure he is, and remarkably famous for his revolutionary techniques in achieving positive outcomes in any possible working environment. He is always in demand by corporate honchos, media moguls, and influential educationists alike. I approached him to be the mentor in your sabbatical, and guess what, he agreed. How could he say no to me! But anyways, that's a long story of a mutually symbiotic relation. For you, it's an opportunity of a lifetime!"

Her disclosure was a sort of paradoxical note for me to react upon.

At one moment, I was in "all praises" for the pianist, who by my wonderful fate was also going to be my mentor. It was getting too complicated for me as whether to confer him with the best accolades from my side or to scrutinise him perfectly for he was going to be my mentor for the whole sabbatical! Finally deciding not to comment upon things, I gave her a thankful gesture and followed her. Albeit I could hardly hear her above all the hubbub in the auditorium, yet I was too sure that very soon she'd be introducing me to Mr. Pathak. Walking through a mob of strangers and greeting them with fake smiles, we finally arrived upon our time to meet the man of the moment. He was mobbed by a lot of people who were applauding his efforts with a hint of something serious brewing intermittently until finally he saw us approaching towards him. He emphatically rushed towards Madam and greeted with a revered look in his eyes for her. I heard him for the very first time.

“In which of the three classes would you place justice: goods desirable in themselves, goods desirables in themselves and for their results or goods desirables for their results only?” Mrs. Sikand was beaming as if wistfully rejoicing the moment until finally she replied in a slightly quivering tone…

“Glaucon! The second one of course! For I am the wisest one alive, for I know one thing and that is that I know nothing.”

“Either we shall find what it is we are seeking or at least we shall free ourselves from the persuasion that we know what we do not know.”

“Come then and let us pass a leisure hour in storytelling, and our story shall be the education of our heroes. And speaking of heroes Mr. Pathak, let me introduce you to the one that we are having with us fortunately. She is ‘Sara Vasistha’ and undisputedly, the best of her cadre.”

I was feeling a bit squeamish and he sensed it immaculately until finally he said.

"Hello Sara! I hope you didn't mind our verbal duel. Well, we have a history of a wonderful learning experience together. These citations of Plato's immortal 'The Republic' used to be one of our favourite topics of contemplation. Ah! The time flies! Honestly, I never thought myself relevant of being a mentor to anyone until she approached me and successfully convinced me of my unconventional approach to things, which we both believe here, could be worthy of passing on to someone as brilliant like you! I am indeed very keen on working with you. Besides, there's always an abundance to learn from an avid young psychologist!"

I saw him briefing and taking control of things in a very eloquent manner. However, I was not yet convinced and decided to dig a bit deeper into the mettle of this somewhat imposed rather than my own chosen mentor.

"Sir, with due respect, I am certainly assured that it'd be an unforgettable learning experience. I am indeed very thankful to Madam for conferring me with such an opportune learning experience. I am sure she'd have toiled much harder to recruit me at your end and I'd always appreciate the same. Yet I am curious to know if her words of praise for me were enough for you to recruit me? I hope you understand what I meant!"

I saw him passing a cursory glance to her and simultaneously giving her a contented smile too. He paused for a moment and then spoke very firmly.

"All of us carry a chip on our shoulders, yet there are very few brave ones who succeed in shaping their turbulent pasts into a refulgent motive for a future of purpose, a future that holds the power to embrace millions of other futures. Seems like a comic book script - turbulent past leading to a heroic future! But it takes courage to convince ourselves for it and that courage can do wonders! I think this should suffice us all, because honestly we are already too late for dinner and I am in no mood of letting my guests go without the scrumptious delicacies. So shall we?"

I saw him advancing and leading us through in a confident gait. I followed them silently as they were sharing their lighter moments. Once again I could not feel my heartbeat for it still yearned to reverberate along the healing music which was hitherto never been experienced by me. Life once again confronted me with an unprecedented threshold and I decided to let it choose its own course this time around too…

Chapter Six

I was invited by Mr. Pathak to his residence cum office in the Vasant Kunj area of New Delhi. It was a bit overwhelming for me to discover a young psychologist managing to have his own residence and office in one of the most expensive residential areas not only in the nation but probably around the globe! As I reached the mentioned address, I saw a grand bungalow amid the lush green lawn of an ideal length measuring approximately one hundred by one hundred square meters, with magnificent flowers blooming, presenting altogether a mesmerizingly enchanting view.

I was enjoying some time alone in the serene ambience until I noticed an alert Beagle puppy wagging its tail, playfully waiting for my consent to join in his mischiefs. The scene reminded me of the tranquility of a piano concert, drawing me back into that trance-like state. The puppy suddenly dashed into the house, only to reappear later, frolicking in the company of Mr. Pathak, who sported a new hairstyle.

"That was a dog whistle he responded so quickly to. His name is Max and he's unbelievably mischievous yet honestly, I am infatuated with him." Mr. Pathak said.

"Certainly, he's an adorable one. I am very much impressed by your collection of flowers. They are so splendid."

"It's your modesty. I have taken special attention to choose the flowers which thrive in the shade. Here you'll find 'lily of the valley', 'Alpine forget-me-not', 'Jacob's ladder', Solomon's Seal', 'Anemone Blanda Blue', 'Lungwort', 'Viola', 'Cowslip Primrose', and 'Tuberous Begonias' to name a few."

"Wow! Had you not been a professional psychologist, you'd have been a successful horticulturist for sure."

"Indeed, my fervour for flowers, particularly for these ones, is because of my belief that one should not be a 'fair-weather' friend. You might find it a bit peculiar, but they never fail to instil that faith in me."

"Well said, Sir. You must be having your faith fortified through such lively and beautiful creations of Nature; yet I was surprised to notice certain other inspirations missing."

He noticed my hands moving nonchalantly through his hair and his contemplative mood suddenly turned to a jovial one as he spoke.

“Aha, you noticed the chopped hair. Well, there’s a plausible psychological explanation for it too, if only you are interested to listen to it.”

“Oh sure! How often do we have psychological explanations for haircuts?”

“God save me from a woman’s sarcasm! But anyways, as you are aware, initially, there was a prevailing theory that inner agents were responsible for a person’s behaviour until the famous discovery was made that the tail of a Salamander would move when touched or pierced even though the tail had been severed from the Salamander’s body. This discovery introduced the concept of external agents influencing human behaviour. The external agent is what we know now as ‘Stimulus’, and the behaviour controlled by it is known as ‘Response’. Together they make a ‘Reflex’.

It was the famous Russian psychologist, I.P Pavlov, who established the relations between these stimuli and responses through his revolutionary techniques. With his experiment to understand and control the secretion of a dog’s saliva, we understood the phenomenon of ‘Conditioned Reflexes’ - a process of the substitution of stimulus to alter behaviour. So, when I had to perform at the piano concert, I was quite aware of the fact that people’s reflexes are conditioned to see and accept an artist, especially a musician, with traditional long hair! But of course, my long hair could never suffice for a terrible piano score, and I continued to practice meticulously. Yet, when

I was on the stage before commencing upon the score, I noticed contently that more than half of the audience had already accepted me through their conditioned reflexes. And the rest is History."

"Yes! I am aware of that tranquil history, and there's no denying the fact that the long hair created an impression of an ardent artist upon me too. Yet, I often contemplate over that impassive look cloaked beyond the harmless façade when applause and encore were ensuing. Did it happen naturally or was that also a part of a 'Conditioned Reflexes' technique?"

"You have the eyes of an observer, Sara! Keep them focused. The path to reality is extremely treacherous. Sometimes you need to be deceitful enough to save the truth for later. After all, it's always about when to blow or not to blow that whistle."

"Indeed, Mr. Pathak! But not all of us are blessed with the wisdom of deliberating our actions. After all, life is all about learning and unlearning, and it's never too late to make a start!"

"Hmmm… It's never too late indeed. It's always about strengthening the impuissant mind and heart, especially for people like us who strive to do it for the sake of others. And then imagine, people blaming us for building houses on the smokes when they are unwilling to rise above their endearing slumber. Now why should one bother about bearing the imaginary carcasses?"

"A leopard can't change its spots! Lives of people are poised over the choices from time to time. It's too ironical that they seek refuge in us to redeem themselves from their erroneous ones. And we usually tread that extra mile alone with no one else to share with our state of minds."

"Well said, dear! I thoroughly agree that it's too lonely a path to tread. I often tend to practice detachment. Yet, living in a world where every benign thing is beaming in its transience, sometimes I fail to comprehend if my detachment is spurious or genuine."

Walking with a firm gait and motionless eyes, as if lost in the lacunas of certain untold stories of his life, he spread open the doors of his office to me.

It was one of the most passionately designed workplaces I had ever witnessed so far. The entire woodwork was of African mahogany, custom-crafted for office work and very methodically planned and placed by its designer. The recessed ceiling, specially designed lighting, leather chairs, and equipment pertaining to the latest in communication technology presented it as an overall executive corporate office. One entire section was dedicated to photography. The walls were covered with random clicks of all the important events which took place in New Delhi in the present decade. Adjoining closely to them was certain personal stuff, which to my best guess, belonged to the staff members.

"This section is very special to me and my team. We have dedicated these walls to our unforgettable and most cherished experiences. Usually, my team members remain in the field with their projects, but whenever we gather, we inscribe a part of our life worth sharing upon this wall."

As I explored further, I found a large single desk and a splendid chair facing the glass window that presented almost the entire view of the lush green lawn beneath. Behind the chair, there was an oil-on-canvas painting of "The Death of Socrates". It wasn't hard for me to surmise that this was Mr. Pathak's desk unless he confessed it himself.

"Well! Needless to mention to an astute observer like you, that's my personal space in the office."

"It's a nice painting in the background, Sir!"

"It's my personal favourite of all the paintings that were hailed and recognised throughout the world till date. When things go beyond the realm of my abilities, I take refuge in this art and try to contemplate why Socrates chose the severe punishment of drinking the hemlock over exile? Although they say that it was his final lesson for his pupils and probably the entire world, but I let my mind delve into his soul and character to seek other possible explanations."

"So what explanations have you sought?"

"It's always the sacrifice that most severely jolts the notions of people. Now if you see this painting closely, the man leaning against the wall is 'Apollodorus'. There's a belief that he was sent away by Socrates for displaying too much grief. The stoic old man sitting at the foot of the bed is shown as 'Plato', the famous pupil of Socrates and the great philosopher himself. The old man in the white robe sitting upright on the bed with one hand extended over the cup of Hemlock and the other one gesturing in the air is depicted as Socrates himself. In this painting, he is surrounded by men of varying ages, the majority of them in great emotional distress. Albeit this masterpiece of 'Jacques Louis David' perceived to have many inaccuracies like not showing the wife of Socrates at that moment and depicting Plato as an old man, who otherwise would have been a young man, yet I give full credit to the artist for capturing the real emotions and decocting out the dispositions of the people he chose to paint impeccably upon his canvas."

"Indeed, Mr. Pathak! The artist has succeeded in etching the ethos of those men upon the canvas, which will never fail to impart the intended admonitions for the masses."

"Very true! These artists were ingeniously gifted to extract the nuances and motifs of human nature and character through their art. Much more capable than us psychologists in conveying the true picture of the human psyche to the ordinary mass. Isn't it ironical that the more you implode in the labyrinths of the ever-shady human heart, the more you succeed in decoding the complexities of the outer enigmatic world, which is what these artists endured with and the result is masterpieces like these!"

"I agree with you. When I see the works of artists like Van Gogh and Michelangelo, I notice that despite their tragic disorders, they bestowed the world something extraordinary that is revered till date."

"Yet agonizingly, the world is as obtrusive as it ever was. This may be a sign of hope or despair as again it ends up to the choice of an individual to opt for the one among the endless array of paths proffered to us by the world we live in."

I saw him contemplating again upon the visage of Socrates in the painting as if aspiring to explore the reasons for choosing Hemlock over exile until I saw a young, petite lady in impressive corporate attire approaching us in a confident manner.

"Excuse me, Sir! It's 11.00 a.m. and you have a meeting with Mr. Jain, M.D. of M/S Jain Corporates at his office in Connaught Palace at 12 noon sharp. You should better be leaving now. All the relevant documents are ready."

"Ah! Ayesha! What would I do without you? Sara, she is Ayesha Tyagi, my right arm indeed, only if there could be the most appropriate corporate jargon for her which I might've coined! But anyways, she manages all the corporate affairs ranging from scheduling the meetings and the proper documentation of research and project-related literature. I am clueless without her. Ayesha, she is Sara Vasishta. She is Hons. In psychology from the prestigious Carmel Institute and has joined us for her sabbatical before commencing her Masters in the same field. A very talented one I must admit! Our small organisation will be richly inherited through her presence and that is my firm belief! Now Sara, pardon me for the day. I want you to spend some time with Ayesha and get acquainted with her. She's a very resourceful one. Very soon I'd be inducting you in your first field assignment."

"Sure, Sir, I'd be looking forward to it."

Moments before the man beseeching for certain philosophical answers was now leaving for the call of a ruthless, pragmatic modern world. I was wondering who was more obtrusive, the world or its people!

Chapter Seven

Ayesha was a shrewd working woman with remarkable professional acumen. No wonder Siddhartha appointed her to manage all the corporate dealings and affairs along with the documentation of the research work safely in the archives, with proper monitoring of patents too. She briefed me on all the relevant details worth knowing about this venture started by Mr. Pathak, which he affectionately named as "Ignis". She also narrated all the major incidents which occurred since the inception of "Ignis" to me. According to her, I was too lucky to be inducted as a team member in this revolutionary organisation as it was something too elusive for all those novice psychologists and experienced ones too, as they might not be exposing themselves to experiences as versatile as here.

It was a pleasant surprise to know that many of the glittering names in the field of Clinical Psychology were somehow associated with the organisation; which, as per their personal opinions, turned out to be a turning point in shaping their careers. It was astonishing to acknowledge a young psychologist as the guiding factor in the paths of the modern prima-donnas of psychology.

My curiosity was, however, partially subsided as Ayesha told me about the educational background of Siddhartha. He was a Ph.D. in Psychology from the University of Oxford. His ingenious methods of understanding the human psyche were unequivocally hailed and recognised in the prestigious institute. Upon his merit alone, he was even offered the post of Assistant Professor in the very last year of his academics, which he did not accept as he wished to serve here first. He knew that here the society is not much aware of the impact and healing powers of Psychology in todays stressed lives. And no one else deserves its service more than a nation like ours.

She also told me that to go skin-deep into the minds of modern Indian mass; he insinuated among them like an insider in the strata of our complex class-driven society. Such intense was his zeal for the truth that his efforts encompassed working as a simple labourer in a steel mill to leading the HR department of an eminent MNC. Deliberately choosing to travel with the masses who could only afford a general compartment of a Train to travelling with CEOs in the economy class of a luxury airliner.

For almost an entire year, he traversed probably the entire nation for his quest to fathom the true being of the modern Indian, which, as per him, was poised beautifully amid the cultural roots and brutal yet pragmatic modernity, until finally he embarked upon his dream of launching "Ignis", with a single-minded notion of serving the people.

Being the lone progenitor of his crusade against the callous approach of society towards the victims of certain mental ailments arising out of extreme working conditions or the dire needs of an individual to keep up the pace with ever-transforming society, he actually, through his compelling research of that one year, influenced the intelligentsia and the affluent ones to support his vision, if not for the welfare then at least for the better output of people, who were an indispensable part of their work and very much responsible for their survival and the survival of their corporate empires.

My induction programme continued until the very next day. The more I learned about this unique venture, the more eager I became of being actively involved in its projects as I was seeing it as a brilliant platform to have a firm grip on the brilliant subject of Psychology, which otherwise is like a treasure lying covertly in deep waters and I could not refrain myself anymore from taking that dip in those deep, abysmal waters.

The next day when I reached there, I found Ayesha too engrossed in her work. There was a certain purity depicting her professional profundity which inhibited me from disturbing her and I decided to wait awhile until finally she noticed me.

"Oh, Sara. How long have you been here? I apologise for letting you wait but the work had piled up a bit."

"It's alright, Ayesha. After all, how often do you see people truly enjoying themselves at their workplaces?"

"Absolutely correct, dear. I love my job and equally feel privileged to be appointed for such a crucial role in here."

"Can I ask you something? Pardon me if I am being intrusive."

"Yeah, sure."

"Have you had any prior experience before this job? It might have been a risky decision to opt for this unique venture considering the risk of abandoning an elusive career if you might have one."

She smiled slyly as if she successfully unraveled my mind.

"As I told you earlier that before the inception of this venture, Mr. Pathak was also an HR head of a global MNC. I was also in the same company and in the same department, serving there as a recruitment manager. Being a master of his field, he sensed precisely that I was not content with the conventional ways being followed there. One fine day he called me up and briefed me his original idea. At that moment, it was a bit dicey for me to go for his idea over my seemingly secure job; yet I took the risk as I had tremendous faith in his vision and I think that faith and risk very much paid off in all possible aspects!"

"Indeed!"

"But you mentioned that you were in a recruitment profile which must have involved a lot of meetings and dealings with people. So how did you manage to confine yourself to the office chores?"

"For anyone, it might seem like paper-pusher stuff, and frankly, earlier it was a bit like the same too; but then Siddhartha trusted me and assigned me the job of maintaining the Research and experience work in the Archive section. It's indeed like a gold mine for any Psychology scholar. Imagine being enlightened by all the knowledge here which is gathered passionately by the team members through sweating their minds out there in the field! But there's a protocol too! You can only read the relevant literature if allowed by the one who submits it. She/he can also take it along while leaving the organisation but with a condition of keeping one copy here for the reference and records purpose."

"But isn't it a bit oligarchical on Siddhartha's part to compel his team members to divulge their works only to him and not others? I mean the reference and records section might only be accessed through his permission alone!"

"Moments like these are always unnerving: You can never know when a sane person can erupt into a chaotic squall." She succeeded in burying the cinders inside and replied politely as if in a monotone.

"I don't think so. In fact, he still leaves that final choice upon them, but I have hardly seen anybody not seeking his recommendations to refine their work. It has always been a rewarding experience for them through his wisdom. And besides, when you're in the field, what lies secured in the Archives is often seen in practice of the beholder, only if you have eyes to grasp it!"

"Interesting. Is that protocol thing applied to Mr. Pathak too? After all, there could be some cases, rather experiences, which he might not have shared with anyone. I am not accusing anyone here, but I am only raising a concern!"

Life is sometimes all about allying yourself with a legion or a faction. Some people may never find their crusade, but I was sure Ayesha had found it in the quest of Mr. Pathak until finally she confirmed it.

"I am afraid to disappoint you Sara but my experience doesn't recount any such incident or experience in the history of this organisation. And let's suppose that even if such cases do exist, then I believe that they better remain uncovered; for we might not be capable enough to handle the profundity of them let alone be a part of their conclusion otherwise they'd not have been in the obscurity. And finally, I think the time is ripe now to brief you about your first field assignment."

Chapter Eight

My first field operation was a research programme in the vast state of Uttar Pradesh where I was involved in seeking authentic reasons as to why the Women lore in the rural areas of the state were bearing a high illiteracy rate over their male counterparts.

Being one of the most densely populated states of the country with a population of nearly about 250 million; the state government officials were concerned over the wide gap of illiteracy between the male and female population of the rural belt. While the overall male literacy rate in the state was 77.28 percent, the female literacy rate was a mere 57.18 percent with more disconcerting figures in the rural areas.

Despite conferring the provincial mass with all the basic amenities requisite for commencing formal basic education, the female population was somewhat uninterested towards educating themselves. We were asked to cover the western area adjoining the Nepal border for this project while other members covered the other areas of a small nation-like state.

Siddhartha chose his most talented and performing chunk for this prestigious project and asked me to be a part of their research and assist them as applicable. We were a team of three members and I was clearly the odd one out for everyone. The other two members namely, "Vivek Pandit" and "Rachna Bhattacharaya" were masters in their fields who had brought various laurels to the organisation.

While anticipating the intensity of the project, I was naturally too nervous and this simmering apprehension faded the curiosity of the archives for the better. Siddhartha advised us to get skin-deep into the rural community by being an integral part of their ethos since being an outsider to them could never bring the intended results to us.

Considering this advice, Vivek framed a plan and as per that, he'd be disguising as a tailor and would project himself as a desperate one who is in dire need of establishing self for the sake of survival and financial support of a big family. Rachna and I were guised as his wife and sister respectively, who had pursued him in his quest and were willingly sharing his burdens, which probably was a common and revered practice in the rural folklore.

It was a simple yet seemingly effective plan. While he dedicated himself to unravel the male psyche, we were accredited to do the more important job. Our preparations commenced a month earlier before finally moving to one of the villages in the district of Pilibhit, which was an apt location for our endeavour. We travelled frequently to our destination in the local transport and joined the locals in their daily chores for the sake of proving ourselves as authentic as possible for the sake of extracting genuine data for the project in hand.

When everything was finally on track and we were seamlessly embarking upon the task, the three of us decided to spend some time together; for in the hustle and bustle, we had bothered the least to know and learn more about each other until finally, we managed to find some time together to unwind.

They started with me, and I strived to maintain the fine balance between my tribulations and the relative revelations. However, I could not veil my inhibition and unwillingness to be more candid about myself, which they very much respected and didn't push me any further for divulging anything that must not be disclosed as per the personal moral code. It was then Rachna's turn who was a master in Clinical Psychology from the prestigious University of Calcutta. Psychology was her first choice and she always wanted to excel in this field. Being a prodigious one, she outdid all her fellow students throughout her academic career. Her family's financial constraints forced her to quit further studies and rather choose a job of a role-identification manager in the Industrial Relations (I.R) department of one of the leading organisations in that domain. The way she was narrating the events so fervently, I was sure that her path too might have crossed with Siddhartha.

'I was deputed as a "Role-Identification" manager in the time of crisis in that esteemed organisation. I knew since its inception that it was a serious responsibility and would probably ask for diligence beyond imagination.

For two painstaking months, I identified the role of every department and designed a model of the "Should be" manpower aligned to the key roles of the department keeping the time frame, finances, development and other crucial factors in mind and then compared it to the existing one.

Based on our research, stern actions were taken, which actually was the demand of the hour too. A lot of reshuffling and manpower redistribution was done with issuing of prior notices to the respective departments. This led to incessant labour and management staff unrest and for the first time in its history, the organisation witnessed a joint strike of labour Union and management staff. Desperate measures were taken to appease the revolting agencies and in times like these, there's always collateral damage.

I and my team members were held responsible for the whole anarchy-like state. To our astonishment, the same people who were hailing us and acknowledged our work as a breakthrough research only a fortnight ago, were now alleging us of a possible collusion with some rival organisations.

Of course, they could not fire me until strong evidence against me could surface so they conspired to prove my findings as a calculation glitch before casting me out. For this, they required confirmation from one of the leading and approved third-party agencies. Mr. Pathak lead "Ignis" was chosen for this job. They offered him a hefty amount to speak against me. I still recall when we interacted in the least favourable of times and his every word still reverberates inside me.

"Do you know it's one brilliant job and least expected from a beginner."

I was in a state of shock and humiliation and didn't want to comment.

"Let me put it in a very simple way for you. These findings are authentic and nobody in the world can prove them false. Ironically, your Management could not reap its benefits in a way they could have, and they turned it into a fiasco. Now they want to appease the people with desperate measures, and firing people like you seems a plausible option to them."

'But what's my fault? I only did my job. If I get fired, it'd be a professional disaster for me.'

"It's not always about seeking faults. Sometimes truth alone does not suffice. You need to learn to not let it divulge to the unworthy and incapable ones like them. I will never report your work as unscrupulous, but believe me; they'd find someone else for it."

'I choked in front of him. That was an abysmal, sinking feeling and equally embarrassing too. But then, in those moments of crisis, he offered me to work for him and on exactly the same pay scale. Initially, I thought it as a honey trap as I believed him to be one of those who sought to destroy me, but then as he told me more about his venture, I started believing in him. Our M.D personally came to thank him for such a peaceful resolution on my part and his last words to him instilled tremendous faith in me, "Sir, one day you'd definitely realise what you lost and what I inherited from your organisation. Frankly, I personally want it to happen very soon." and from that day onwards I never looked back and never repented my decision too.

Her countenance was similar to that of a Knight who breathes an air of ethereal contentment meriting the value of his every action even in the eyes of adversity. Vivek and I left her to the silence of her thoughts momentarily for what could not be expressed further on her part, let it be divulged to the cloak of the night.

Vivek Pandit was a professor of Clinical Psychology at the prestigious Banaras Hindu University (BHU). His career was illustrious. He was self-motivated and deeply content with his chosen field. He was famous in the University for achieving the highest percentage of students attending his lectures. He was also called upon numerous times by the Government investigation agencies to unravel the strangely twisted criminal minds. It was through his impeccable judgements that the law could impart true justice to numerous cases of inscrutable sociopaths.

Like almost all brilliant minds, he too shared a turbulent past which compelled him to abandon his glorious future as a professor and knock upon the doors of Mr. Pathak, the only one he could find to have answers to his predicament.

"When my loving wife committed suicide, on that fateful day I didn't have the slightest inkling that she was unhappy and would succumb to her persuasive inner darkness. She suffered from bouts of stupor initially. When diagnosed, she was found to have Bipolar II disorder. It was hard to believe that beyond her smiling face, she was veiling such enduring pain silently. In her dark days, she suffered frequently from depressive episodes, suicidal thoughts, and shorter intervals of well-being. Bipolar II was always one tough ailment to be diagnosed. Her family mistook it for high functional behaviour or merely a personality attribute. We were told to be as servile as it possibly could to her unrealistic behaviour. I was very firm and confident that one day my love would reach her, albeit I could see it in her eyes, the way she was losing patience with herself and with the people closely knit.

As time passed, there was a remarkable improvement in her. The primary psychologist was very sure of her being normal again and eventually, he referred her to be sent back home for some time in a hope of quick healing; which was obvious on his part too. I was enthused by her will to choose life over her inner demons and was confident of a successful treatment until one day she committed suicide at home. On that fateful day, I failed to discern a single sign of depression or anxiety on her serene face before leaving for my lectures. Later, from her personal stuff, we found a diary revealing to us that she was never well and all of that was her brilliant façade to her relentless urge of ending her life at home and not in some hospital."

"I will never be able to forgive myself for that. All of my academics, achievements, research et al seemed too futile and non-functional to me, and I was almost on the verge of giving up on this career until finally one of my colleagues told me about Siddhartha. I wrote to him and he instantly responded. Through him, I came to know that cases like my wife were very scrupulously studied and researched for hundreds of man-hours in the Western nations to seek conclusive reasons for the astonishing fact that patients over there too had actually fooled the most seasoned of Psychiatrists and then committed suicide. He informed me about the peculiar concept of 'Micro expressions and micro Gestures.' He narrated to me in-depth some very similar yet famous cases as to how the seemingly docile mental state of the patients was actually a remarkable deceit which only surfaced through the knowledge of these micro expressions and gestures. I was literally dwarfed by the enormous power of the human mind. My loss was irrevocable yet it bestowed me a reason to persist and explore relentlessly, a motive to heal millions like my wife out there left to be suffered in their own mental filth.

All three of us endured an afflicting past, the past whose memories etched its perpetual melancholy in our hearts forever. But it was unfair to say that this dysphoria only contributed miseries to our lives. It invigorated too, that inexorable urge to unmask the covert powers of the human mind. Being silent in those fading hours of the night, we knew that this personal crusade was for the sake of millions, but somehow we were selfish too; for it assuaged the unbearable pain of human vulnerability, ironically our vulnerability."

Chapter Nine

Vivek had already segued himself perfectly into the ethos of the village community. He disguised himself impeccably as a skilled tailor, and his incomparable diligence to mingle with people led him to become an important and inseparable member of the local community. I was amazed to find that such was the impact of his benign presence, that more and more people started to flock around his shop in their leisure time to narrate experiences and other important aspects of their lives.

Rachna and I succeeded in seeking out a suitable job for ourselves, which kept us close to the vicinity of the village women, and that was our prime objective too. Since our chosen village was very close to the Nepal Border, we discovered that the women over there were keeping themselves engaged in one common job. It was a simple yet tiring work of transferring consumables and other household items from one side to another. The business people in the village used to sell their goods across the border, and those women were actually the medium of delivering them on a daily basis through either bicycle or by foot. The already experienced ones were capable of making more than ten rounds across the territory while their male counterparts kept themselves engaged in agriculture or other suitable jobs.

Moreover, this was the usual lifestyle of the people of the rural belt of our research interest. We could not blame them, especially women, for opting for that tedious job over preferring to educate themselves since none of them wanted to leave their villages, and education for them meant a passport to the outer world; besides, whatever they were doing here was lucrative too. Initially, Rachna and I faced a very tough time in matching ourselves to their daily chores. The majority of the women were fit and physically very strong. Since they were capable of completing a minimum of three rounds, both of us were giving up after one, as obviously, none of us was habitual to this rigorous job of carrying such heavy loads on bicycles and covering long distances. Much to our further mockery, we became a laughing stock to them for our poor working efficiency and dismal outputs. Yet, we used this mockery as a stepping stone of healthy camaraderie, and in return for our patience, we got acquainted with them successfully, and they too started offering their support for our enhanced daily outputs.

The basic tenet of contemporary psychology states that an individual's mental health is largely dependent upon a good social network. We discovered that despite being endowed with such sparse resources of a developed lifestyle, the mass of those country lands had emerged as mentally very strong over their urban counterparts. To a large extent, their mutual dependence was the major reason for their survival as they transcended the bitterness of differences for the benefits of symbiotic survival.

That resilient urge of not giving up on their cherished beliefs seemed frozen like lost time inside their imperturbable eyes and rigid faces. Staying there for over two months, we gathered enough experience to formulate valuable data to be submitted to the government authorities and for them to ponder upon the basic loopholes and failures of their efforts in successfully educating the rural belt or what possible measures must be taken to influence them for a much-deserved change to make themselves ready for a fierce modern world out there, a world which was secretly lurking to pounce upon their cherished folklore. It was hard to decide if it was better to educate them or to leave them to their own choices. But the devouring of their rudimentary lifestyle through the modern world was imminent, and education alone was their only hope of their safe survival.

We planned to extend our stay for a maximum of one month more to compile our work and move on to other endeavours. With every passing day, I could see Vivek hastening things up and creating a notion in the minds of villagers that he'd have to leave the place for the sake of attending to an emergency call back home. I was astonished to see his influence over the villagers in such a short time when they actually started visiting our house proffering any possible support they could help him with in his personal emergency.

During one such day of passing sympathies, he spoke to both of us.

"We'd be leaving exactly after seven days. With the development of our work, I assume further delay will be futile. Still, if anyone of you wishes to extend the stay, I am ready for that."

I could see certain inhibitions holding Rachna until I decided to take the lead.

"There's this young and bright girl whose name is 'Swati'. She is eighteen and has recently been admitted to the local degree college. We met her during our daily job, and our friendship grew thicker with time. She's a promising young woman who deserves to take a leap forward in her life. But her parents are firm about her marriage this year. They have even found a suitable match for her."

"Oh, you must be talking about Deenanath's daughter. Indeed, she's a bright young lady. Her father narrated to me numerous tales of her academic excellence and a resolute will to afford her own education. But marriage is her choice too. Nobody is forcing her to do that, I suppose."

"But you know how things are here, Vivek. She must have succumbed to her family's decision. Once she gets married, I believe that'll be the end of the road for her aspirations."

"What do you wish to do, Sara?"

"I want to have a word with her personally. I'd inspire her to reconsider her decision even if there's a potential threat of family disdain! I don't want to see her giving up on her dreams."

"Fair enough. Take your time. My advice though is to be cautious and always keep in mind that you are not sort of a crusader or renegade for transforming their lives. These simple and serene people have a very firm hold on their ethos, which they won't give up that soon and neither will they allow any foreign intervention."

"I promise you, Vivek, there won't be any audacity on my part. I'd deal with this with complete peace and wisdom."

And so I decided to intervene in her life on a very serious note. I was anticipating that right moment, until one day we got ourselves a forced day off due to the transportation strike leaving us with no job in hand for the entire day. Rachna allowed me to do it myself, and I admired her decision. Swati and I planned to spend the rest of the day at her place, and I knew this was the right moment.

While she was too keen to show me her valuable childhood possessions kept tenderly as souvenirs of her dearest memories, I was too anxious to commence that worthy discussion with her about reconsidering her decision of an early marriage and seeking out ways to procrastinate it for the better. Amid the mounds of her cherished possessions, I found a dusty edition of "Panctantra", an ancient collection of animal fables to inculcate morality and other important lessons of life.

I picked it up and started with her.

"So this one is precious too!?"

"Of course. I still remember these fables being narrated fondly to us in our hassle-free childhood. I have inherited a lot of wisdom from it."

I leaned forward, my eyes wide with sincerity as I spoke. "That's true. I too heard these stories in my childhood from mother. But you know, sometimes I feel that stories like these get faded away in the dusty recesses of the pages with time. And their true inheritance never gets accomplished by anyone."

Rachna shook her head firmly, her voice rising slightly in her conviction. "No! That's an absolutely false notion on your part. I always acknowledged them in my life and they never failed me. People usually give up on these when falling prey to their own vulnerabilities at the crossroads of their lives and then end up blaming every pious thing as a mirage of a possible source of strength."

I tilted my head, a frown creasing my brow. "Don't you feel that you are standing on one such crossroad of your life too? And have sort of failed to discern that source of strength?"

Swati blinked, taken aback. "I am sorry, I didn't get you precisely."

I forced my expression to soften, but kept my tone firm. "Let me be very honest with you, Swati. I don't acknowledge your decision of getting married too soon at all. You should pursue your education rather than all this. I strongly condemn your decision to give up on your dreams for the sake of your family."

"But that's not true, Sara." Swati's voice was earnest, her hands gesturing openly. "My husband and his family have vowed not to be a hindrance in my educational prospects. In fact, they support my decision."

I raised my eyebrows skeptically. "Do you seriously believe they'll support you later? You know very well how seriously prejudiced these people are towards imparting education to women after their marriage. What if they refuse to educate you out of their predispositions? Do you wish to cover your entire life paddling the bicycle?"

I was expecting an anxious response from her side, but her countenance was rather far from being apprehensive at all. Mustering that hidden wisdom out of her repository of experiences, she spoke something that was least expected from her side.

"We village folks are very simple ones, dear sister. If there's one inheritance that probably all of us have in common; it's that we tend to be content with whatever life bestows us with. It'd be too erroneous to say that this life has always disappointed us. We know how to unveil happiness in tribulations. If today I am doing this tiring job of delivering goods, then it's also true that it is the sole medium of educating myself and would remain in the near future also. When my family tried to interrupt my education due to financial constraints, then life bestowed me this path to pursue my education. Difficult it was, but I am content that it conferred me the path. And this is my true inheritance from life, not to discriminate among the paths to our dreams. If in the future, my households decide to disrupt my education dreams, then again I'd patiently seek and wait for the new path from life, which I am sure will not disappoint me this time too and would confer me with another one."

I felt helpless to utter a single word to her simplicity. But with a trembling voice, I asked her. "Why do you always wish to tread upon the more arduous paths when life is offering you other, more plausible options?"

"Sara, to me, a path is a path. I don't know much about you, but I've this strong feeling that you wish to make my path less severe. To me, you are also a sort of path shown by life. It's remarkably strange that until yesterday, I was in the doldrums about pursuing my dream of education after marriage but now after talking to you, I felt like life has communicated to me again and has urged me to not give up. It's enough for me now to take that leap of faith. But whosoever you are and wherever you are destined to reach, keep on inspiring the people in distress. You have that power in you."

Once again, I was in a state of complete delirium blended with the feeling of abandoning myself to her innate wisdom towards life. I hugged her out of pure affection and wished all of the world's happiness to her. For the rest of the days, I spent my maximum time with her. We had wonderful discussions as we shared our perceptions about this weird world. Never did I dare disclose my tribulations to her, but I believed that somehow she had already surmised about my enduring life too.

The time finally came when we bid adieu to that wonderful village, which entrusted not only inestimable wisdom but also unforgettable relations. My first project was a grand success, and my work was thoroughly appreciated. I spoke in detail to Siddhartha about my work but never mentioned Swati to him during our long discussions.

Before starting up with an altogether new one, I asked for a few days off which he gladly accepted. As I was about to leave, he asked.

"Hey, Sara, if there's something you wish to add to that photography section, you are welcome to do so."

I turned back and saw a kind of look that meant, "I've been there too."

I scurried along the photography section and posted my snap with Swati over there. I was expecting him to ask about her, but instead, I saw him glued to the portrait of Socrates with Hemlock in his hands.

Chapter Ten

It was a gentle refuge as I spent a week back home. I was rejuvenated and yearning to embark upon a new project. It was a positive sign as my inclination towards the sabbatical was more fervent than ever, which was something to my sheer astonishment, really unexpected to happen so soon.

Upon reaching the office, Ayesha greeted me very fondly.

"Ah, welcome back! Congratulations for the brilliant job in your very first project. You literally surpassed many expectations indeed, not shy to say mine too. Needless to mention though, but you seem quite a natural to me."

"Oh, Ayesha. It's too big an assumption to make yet. I've just started by the way. But honestly, had it not been Vivek's astute vision and focused leadership, we'd not have achieved as desired."

"Of course, dear. Vivek has always been brilliant yet I've seen newbies losing their nerves every now and then to similar situations. But you were firm and that's a very good sign. Well, as the deeds speak for themselves; Mr. Pathak has offered you a new project. The exciting part is that you'd be doing it all alone. You're lucky, Sara. Haven't seen anyone grabbing an independent one so soon for a while; but then you deserved it too."

I was a bit edgy as well as exuberant when I heard about the independent one being rolled towards me. I sort of suppressed my feelings and behaved as conventionally as I possibly could.

"But, Ayesha, don't you think it's a bit too early for me? I mean there'd be definitely other more deserving ones than me."

She passed me a stern, exploring glance as if sensed my intentions clearly.

"First of all, it isn't like any corporate, government or business-related project, so there's not much hassle and precautionary measures to be taken care of. We needed a truly talented fresher for the same, and the first choice was obviously you. When Siddhartha declared that you'd be handling it all alone, everybody endorsed his decision, so there's no question of any biases too. Now if you don't mind, I'd like to brief you about this new project and acknowledging your consent as well as a part of the protocol."

Ezekiel College of Management was one of the most sought-after colleges of the nation for pursuing management studies. Governed by the Christian Missionary Society, the college was an epitome of imparting world-class education aligned to ethical management to the students who got themselves enrolled there. No wonder, the alumni of the college were among the leading industrialists, CEOs, and management gurus who were not only masters of their fields but also kindled and encouraged the possibility of an ethical business environment in times of pervading unethical practices in almost every aspect of the modern business environment.

The Dean of the college, Father Daniel Howard, recently met Siddhartha and expressed his grave concern over the decadence of the notion of ethics and a sense of business morality in the minds of youth in that prestigious institution.

Being a prominent public figure, Father Daniel was not an orthodox preacher. He was aware of the modern, callous times and always believed in seeking a pragmatic approach to the issues of modern society. One of his insightful traits was to inculcate and perpetuate a fine balance of ethics and management among the students who are going to be the potential leaders of tomorrow in their respective chosen fields.

Ayesha told me that Siddhartha often visited the college to comprehend the gravity of the situation. As per him, the issue was of grave concern yet it could be resolved. Someone, probably of their age, needs to insinuate an antidote of that elusive fine balance in their novice yet capable minds against such contagious notions and that someone needs to be very sharp and discreetly motivated. All of it demanded a subtle treatment as there was always a risk of failure, which eventually could turn the antidote into an apathetic mindset.

I was also told that he left the final choice upon me to make or break the project as he always confers to whoever he proposes as worthy of it to lead.

"Ayesha, I am a bit confused about the reality. Before making up my mind for the final decision, I want to meet Father Daniel personally. Can you please fix an appointment with him?"

"He was right. He told me that you'd not accept the proposal before meeting with the Father yourself. I have already arranged the same. Tomorrow at 11.00 a.m. sharp."

I sensed genuine accolades yet a servile attitude in her eyes for him but I was definitely not amused. For me, it was a logical decision which should have been made by any sane person while making the final decision. I replied to her curtly which might have offended her but then why should I fake my intentions in expressing something genuine.

"That's better, Ayesha. Any sane person in authority might have done the same. Tomorrow at the stipulated time, I'd be visiting Father Daniel and on the basis of my rendezvous with him, I'd be able to determine my future course of action on this project."

"Sure, Sara. As always, the final call would be yours alone."

So, I went to visit the dean at the arranged time. The campus premises pervaded inside me certain nostalgia of my own college days. Being smitten by that unexpected hysteria, I decided to saunter around the college with a thought of catching a brief glimpse of the looming decadence which was a potential threat to the prestigious institute.

To my cursory observation, I found nothing peculiar to be treated as a threat as envisaged by Father Daniel and Siddhartha. But then I decided to meet him without any further delay for more lucidity.

As I entered his office, I saw a slender figure in an impressive black cassock too engrossed in his thoughts. His stern, impassive mien was only exacerbating the current crisis, if only there were any to be dealt with.

I gently knocked and spoke politely to pull him out of his stupor-like state.

"Excuse me, Father. May I please come inside?"

A normal person would have experienced a gentle shudder to this sudden bother, but he only rolled his eyes to me and nodded with his approval.

"Sir, my name is Sara Vashist. I have come from 'Ignis' with a due appointment."

"Yes, welcome Sara. I was expecting you anytime now. Please have a seat."

"Thank you very much, Sir."

"My pleasure, Sara. Well, Siddhartha is a very good friend of mine. When I approached him with this current predicament, I was expecting that he'd handle it himself. But then he told me about you and assured me of a definite solution. He praised your zeal for making the positive change."

"Right now, Father, I very much feel like admiring yours. You have done a splendid job in consistently retaining the good reputation of this prestigious institute while balancing it with your personal austere attributes. I could feel the strength of your pious endeavours emanating from this institute."

"It's your modesty, Sara. In fact, the entire missionary society is responsible for this success. It could never be one man's work. But right now, we are feeling somewhat threatened and helpless to conserve it."

"Excuse me, Sir. But before meeting you I roamed around the campus to have an estimate of this threat you are concerned with, yet I could not point out any such. I found things normal; nothing incongruous to be considered as a threat."

"The reason why I've never been conservative in life is due to the fact that things can be truly inculcated, only if accepted through free will. But things are different this time."

"Father, I'd like you to elucidate in-depth."

"There's a very beautiful verse in the Bible that says,

"And be not conformed to this world:

but be ye transformed by the renewing of your mind,

that ye may prove what is that good,

and acceptable,

and perfect, will of God."

To me, change or transformation has always been God's communication for us to decipher his will from time to time. All through my life, I successfully endured these transformations, which were bitter to swallow initially but with time I construed them as the motif of his will, which undoubtedly was for the better alone. It's always been tough to recognise my role in such transformations yet by grace; I succeeded in seeking mine until this moment. Now it's something beyond my realms of comprehending things."

"Please share the reason for your apprehension, Father."

"In the previous year, a very bright and ardent student got enrolled in the College to pursue his MBA in HR. As talent never remains hidden for long, his too was soon discovered through his academics and lucid ideas. Everyone was awe-inspired by his eloquence and command over things in totality. He fetched numerous laurels for the college and has been the consistent topper of the University too."

"That's great, Father. But where's the threat in all this?"

"It's an acceptable truth, Sara, that normal people follow the standards set by the extraordinary ones. His ways of achieving excellence have seriously questioned our conventional methods to strive for the balance of ethics and success."

"How is that possible?"

"His convictions and perceptions are that of an atheist, a nihilist, someone who's achieving one laurel after another not because of any obsession with fame or success but for deriding the way things are civic in society. He is a transformer for sure but his ways are too complex for students to discern. I can see it, Sara, that one day he'd strike the right chord. He'd succeed in seeking that one true connection which binds everything else. Yet I am concerned for those who are chasing him in his blinding, fierce ordeal. They may not be that apt to penetrate deep into things and might lose their purpose along."

"But then there's nothing you can possibly do Father. It's their free will to chase him."

"Yes dear, it's their free will. But I am responsible for the repercussions of their free will, for I have vowed to make them better people for society. I can't see my students losing their paths amid this tormenting cacophony of a crusader."

"Father, it won't be that easy to alter their will. This must be left upon them alone as per my honest sense of judgement.

You cannot stop them from following this prodigy of your institution until he formally leaves it or abandons his ways, which seems far less a possibility. Even then, I believe that his ideas would have sort of incepted too deep in the minds of students by now."

"Yes, you are right. Siddhartha and I faced similar conundrums while arriving at a breakthrough. We postulated numerous possibilities but all in vain. Until we realised that the best solution is to purify the source itself."

"What source? And how to purify it?"

"To inspire the mindset of youth from refraining to deride the civic, we'd have to metamorphose the mind of their inspiration. We'd have to reform their ideal, which can possibly be done through comprehending his ways, his reasons for such deriding notions towards society, to sort of know him inside out and then to mend him entirely by showing him the flaws of his nihilism, his chosen path."

"And you want me to do this through becoming their teacher?"

"An influential one. That's the best way possible, if only you have another idea to tackle the situation."

"Right now I cannot postulate any. But I'd like to get skin-deep into the crisis."

"Any help from my side?"

"For one week, I'd like to be their guest lecturer on Corporate Social Responsibility. I'd be forming an insight into their minds through narrating them the success stories of the organisations which respected and successfully implemented the moral or ethical business model in their working. Albeit my real intentions would be to sense the level of inception and chances of mending things back to normalcy. My choice to pursue as a lecturer or to derive an altogether new idea would solely depend upon the outcome of this one week."

"Fair enough Sara. I'd make the formal note and inform everyone concerned."

Corporate Social Responsibility (CSR) was an obvious choice for me as a guest lecturer since I found it within the realms of psychology and to have grasp upon easily. Yet, before commencing upon this idea of being a guest lecturer in one of the leading institutes of the country, I needed to be meticulous with the intricacies of the chosen subject. Of course, I could not fake it for a longer duration. So, I decided to prepare myself meticulously enough for a week and thought to achieve the impossible- to wrap up with the project itself within these seven days.

I kept mum about this foolhardy idea of mine. For me, it was either these seven days to metamorphose this source or it was never. Keeping this in mind, I designed my plan for the possibly most enduring seven days which I might have come across in very recent times.

I deliberately kept the scope of maximum time for discussions apart from imparting them the basics of CSR, as my real purpose was to comprehend their perspectives and alter them in conformity. I asked Father Daniel for a fortnight to delve thoroughly before embarking on this project, which he accepted without any issues.

I toiled hard and gathered as much information as I possibly could until finally, I was mentally prepared to take this arduous mental maze.

On the very first day of my lecture, I was surprised to be greeted with the full strength of the class, noting not even a single absenteeism. My silent heart whispered, "This has to be today, the magic must happen now."

And so I commenced with my first formal lecture. I spoke fluently about the concept, scope, approaches and importance of the subject model by citing numerous case studies for a better understanding. As decided earlier, I involved student opinions in the end through inciting a very thought-provoking topic. It aimed to question the relevance of keeping business ethics in times of choosing between targets or ethics. It wasn't too hard for me to find out my source which I hoped to purify within these seven days. He was very compelling, harsh and an eloquent speaker. He possessed the ability of devouring the minds of people without any mercy. In his eyes, I saw the frozen truth of a long-enduring past that was the source of his strength and a possible vulnerability too.

At the end of day one, I was finally convinced of the herculean task I had to do. I decided to meet Father Daniels to assure him that his concerns were very genuine.

"So Sara, how was your day?"

"So far it has been good father. I hope you might have received the feedback by now."

"I have received a positive one. So did you find him?"

"You were correct father. He is compelling; deeply motivated and unfathomable. Practically shows no remorse for crushing anyone against his perceptions. I must admit, the students mustn't be blamed for falling into such an abyss of a personality."

"Shashwat Abkari is the only heir of the famous "Abkari Group of Companies". It's a conglomerate of more than thirty different organisations ranging from powerful media houses to steel rolling mills. His father and chairman of the conglomerate, Mr. Vishwamitra Abkari is an alumnus of this very institute. He visited me at the time of his son's admission. I was informed that Shashwat made it to almost all leading B-schools in the world through his merits alone, yet it was his personal decision to pursue his management studies through the same institute from where his father did."

"Do you surmise any particular reason or link of any sort?"

"No, Sara. That was a moment of immense pride for me. Above all, who could have expected such actions from a billionaire's heir for God's sake. You've seen things around nowadays. It's too odd for a person like him to contemplate upon the society, its order and other thought-provoking concerns."

"You are absolutely right, Sir. Yet there must be a very strong reason for a person bestowed with such illustrious a fate to contemplate and all and that reason, Father that very reason is the key to this maze."

As I left his chamber, I was too certain that if I wished to decipher that reason, I'd have to confront him myself as soon as it could possibly be.

So I decided to involve myself seriously in the student discussion section of the lecture for the remaining ones.

With every passing day, the lectures went deeper into the subject and me into his mind. On his every valid point, there was always a fierce opposition from my side until there were only two of us left with no formal winner or loser of the debate.

On the fourth day, our discussion ended as usual but this time on the topic of "Triple Bottom Line," which meant People, Planet, and Profit. As expected from him, he was against the belief that certain profits should be sacrificed to fair and ethical business practices. According to him, the corporation as a whole should be responsible only to their shareholders and to a certain extent only towards society. No profit should be compromised for any ethical or fair practice as organisations are already doing too much for society by conferring lacs of jobs and donating the hard-earned profits would always be at a cost of margins, something that we all are hanging to these days.

I, however, defied his beliefs through real case studies which proved that there's always a scope for mutual existence of profits and ethics, the only concerning point being an intention to kerb the organisation's avarice. As the discussion ended, I saw a blend of squirm and gratification on his face. For any psychologist, such a face was like a tormenting riddle that'll compel him to bolster his efforts and run that extra mile for that elusive breakthrough.

I too was no exception in this regard. And, for my implacable urge to get the truth out of his throat, I played discreetly and looked deeper into his eyes without blinking and with a slight fleer aimed solely to deride his firm, established regulations of mind.

I was sure that this gesture of mine would penetrate him to the core and he'd definitely give up something valuable.

As I was brooding over my next move in the chamber with time running out of my hands, I saw him entering into my cabin. I pretended to be as composed as I possibly could when deep inside I knew that it was the moment of blitzkrieg for both of us. I waited for him to make the first move.

"May I come in, Madam?"

"Yes sure, please."

"Thanks. I hope I might not be spoiling your leisure time. Actually, I thought that a doubting Thomas must also be allowed to speak his mind."

“But I thought he always did. After all, the world doesn’t get influenced that easily. You always need to open up to it. By the way, you can call me Sara.”

“Well Sara, the world will find its way. It always has managed it at last. Ironically, the world and its people have always been crippled to walk on their own. They should actually be indebted to those who could carve out their own paths for others to follow.”

“Indeed. But there should always be a sense of responsibility towards them. When your existence starts to influence more than your own world, you should be cautious enough to retain the order.”

“There’s no order of a morally lopsided society. It will always fall to its own interests in guise of survival, the most common alibi. So here I am, with my idea of screwing the order for the sake of profits and other monetary charms. Let people choose.”

“Why being gratified to see men turning to wolves and gorging upon the remaining morsels of goodness?”

“An arrow has been shot and there’s no turning back for this society now. Can’t you feel its fluidic motion permeating anarchy? Your society has made its choice to doom and I have chosen to be an active catalyst. Nothing personal Sara. I am just a little bit loose on patience.”

“You must be having very strong reasons to wear this crown of thorns.”

"Crown of thorns. The days of Messiah descending to save us are as hypothetical as this very order. Let them be in books, at least they serve a wishful heart."

"Your realisations are those of an unflinching soul enduring pain. When the pain becomes you, such inheritance follows. But sometimes, your pain can heal millions of others. You've that power in you and that's not because you are a billionaire's only heir, but you are among the rarest who could mold their agonies into a fuel for the burning fire inside. Come back, Shashwat, before it's too late... Come back before your forced nihilism devours the kindness away... This world is in dire need of people like you."

"You know Sara, the moment you chose to intervene in and confront my perceptions; I speculated that you are not here for merely delivering the lectures. I was right I suppose. Your observations are correct. You've very astutely determined that I've endured pain; yet this pain has been my unflinching, stalwart companion. If today I am at the threshold of making that final choice of being a saviour or the annihilator of this fleeting order, it's through this pain alone. Undoubtedly, the society has heaved a million reasons out for me to think seriously over the annihilation, yet I have not lost my reverence towards just. I should respect the efforts of any individual who confronts my path and implores for the sake of saving the sinking ship. But then everything comes for a price. The world would have to prove me if it's worth my efforts to try and be on the other side."

And then he left my chamber. I was happy to discern a flickering hope of humanity still burning inside him, braving the cruel winds of his nihilism. But then it was too early to say on whose side his pain was. It was like the similar pain which forged me to what I was today.

I never felt myself so powerful yet so miserably vulnerable at the same moment. For the next two lectures, I didn't participate in the discussions but watched him keenly when he was shredding the conventions of susceptible minds with disdain.

I saw bouts of an insatiable monster waiting desperately to be unleashed yet I could also see, every time when he stared into my eyes, that flickering hope of humanity that was beseeching me to deliver him, preclude him from the unthinkable.

By the end of my sixth lecture, I was ready with my make or break plan and with the zeal of warriors of the first wave, I went to him and elaborated.

"As you said earlier, that you still keep that reverence for just. There's a place I'd like you to see for yourself. Interestingly, pain is also peculiarly poised between the good and bad forces like we all are in our lives. It also hangs loosely, struggling to be on the right side, eagerly awaiting for the right to deliver itself…"

"If there's a nook like that, it's worth paying a visit to…"

"Very well. Tomorrow at the end of lecture, we'd be leaving for that very much alive and rolling nook."

We left after the end of the lecture as planned. While I was ruminating upon my last day and its passing hours for reforming a cynic, a deep, somewhat impatient voice echoed through my mind.

"So, where exactly are we going?"

"Well, I think you must be aware of the 'Army Wives Welfare Association' commonly termed as AWWA. Today we'd be visiting one of their bravest projects named 'AAHWAAN'. My mother works for AWWA and is currently in the administrative role of this project. I spoke to her, and she has made necessary arrangements for us to visit and explore."

"Yeah, I've heard of AWWA. It's an NGO for the comprehensive well-being of Army wives and children. Interesting, you hail from an Army background."

"My father was in the elite 9 Para Regiment of the Indian Army until his death in the Kargil War. Mother was offered this job, and then we got settled here for better."

"Oh. I am extremely sorry…"

"It's alright. Talking of this project that we'd be visiting, it was established in the year 2005 and is currently a successful women empowerment project."

"That's brave. It'd be nice to meet your mother too."

"Well, she left for some prior engagements. She's a very busy woman indeed. But I never complained as we have learned through our own ways, to take cognizance of one another's importance in our lives."

And once again I delved into the realms of my contemplation, and this time he too seemed too lost in his own. For the rest of the journey, we remained silent, as if both of us knew that sometimes the best option is to flow, let things happen on their own, for vulnerability is also sometimes like bliss if heeded sincerely.

Finally, we made it to our destination, and there we were fondly greeted by the peers and other subordinates of Mama. As per my intentions, I wanted to let him experience the whole project alone, hence I contrived myself away.

"Shashwat, Mom wanted me to attend to something important over here. It'd take a minimum of two to three hours. The staff is cooperative and would brief you about the functional operations and other engagements pertaining to the project. I hope you'd pardon me for some time."

"Oh, sure. I'd manage myself."

So I left him to his own wisdom towards something enduringly pious.

"AAHWAAN" was a rehabilitation program solely dedicated to the war widows, needy, and differently abled women. It was a very brave move for the sake of preserving the sanctity of women, as it proffered them a chance in life to build their destiny through their own hands.

The women were engaged in the commercial production of wax candles, paper bags, and other tasks such as designing, stitching, and block printing of fabric. I returned to the site, or more precisely to him, exactly after three hours and found him standing with his arms folded, gazing meditatively at the working women. Calmly, I stood beside him without uttering a word until he noticed my presence, which seemed to breach the subtle nuances of his seemingly arid mind.

His demeanour was emanating his loneliness so clearly that I felt sort of guilty for exposing him to such excruciating and extreme scenarios. It was beyond my vigour to face him, a vigour which was nothing but a culmination of a similarly testing life like the one I was leading too…

I decided to leave then when I realised that a firm hand clasped my wrist, and an unabashed, sonorous voice shattered the smothering silence that was often very rare between us.

He pitched his voice low and solemn as he shared his heartache. "You know the love of my father's life, the love for which he risked losing everything, the only relation that completed him and he too revered the most, my dearest mother… She died in a mental asylum." he paused, his eyes distant as he remembered, "In her last moments, I was there beside her deathbed. The only thing I could figure out of her immovable gaze upon me in that final hour of her life was that even her love could not bring my father back to us, that even the most sacred and strong relations get smashed to smithereens when exposed to the brutal codes of reality and survival, that there's no judgement impending for this society but to let it rot in its own filth.

I swear upon my mom's last enduring gaze, I could never have forgiven this society including myself until today. Today, I saw hundreds of those gazes again. Today, I realised what she really wanted to say to me in those last moments of hers.

"Look around! In this honourable, conscientious herd of women, there are few who lost everything to war and if life could not have got more, they were robbed of the grants too which were granted to them for their husband's sacrifices by none other than their own households."

I shook my head slowly, "When I asked them don't they feel betrayed and wish for the society to perish? They calmly replied that society should strive for harmony. Above all, they've forgiven those callous households too, as these venerable women believe that a person's life is nothing but repercussions of his choices. Those who betrayed them in their darkest hours did it out of their choice while they decided to forgive them and fight on till the end, out of their choice."

A trace of irony touched his voice, "Isn't it ironical that even after all of it, they wish to see their kids serving for the Army? To comprehend that abysmal gaze of my mother that devoured out every ounce of sanity out of me, I decided to live my father's life in a more reprehensible manner than he could ever imagine. I wanted to see how love gets faded upon the altar of priorities. I wanted to be inflicted with those tribulations through which the heart undergoes when forced to make that final call between dreams or reality. I wished to see myself being incinerated by that frozen, vacillating gaze that got etched forever in my heart; but then I couldn't, not after seeing all this here…

Today I have finally deciphered that final heritage of my mother. I don't know who you are and who asked you to alter my course of life and for what possible interests, believe me, I won't even ask you but I'd like to thank you for taking me closer to the truth of my life. This time, I won't sacrilege her trust. Her daughter would not commit the same mistakes lest someone else be morphed with the walls of an asylum again."

My eyes were glinted, and my throat was parched. Words could not muster the courage to soothe him in his moment of realisation. He stared deeply into my eyes, and I saw his monster breathing its last in the dark recesses of his own misconceptions, which were incidentally the real progenitor of it…

I smiled out of triumph and elation, seeing a staunch, brave individual being resurrected for a new epoch.

Chapter Eleven

Within a short span of seven days, I was successful in transforming an inveterate mind. It was a moment of triumph, with distinctions pouring in from everywhere. Father Daniel was flabbergasted, and he termed it as something close to a "Divine Intervention" and lauded me for achieving something very close to impossible. Flattery would have been too fusty an act to be expected from a person of his stature, but he was seriously interested in inducting me as a full-time faculty at the esteemed institute. I, however, was not considering myself worthy of the same and rather opted to decline the proposal politely. He blessed me for the life ahead and assured that the college's doors will always be open for me in the future for any personal or professional help.

When I landed in the office after almost a gap of a month, I wasn't aware that Siddhartha and other team members had arranged a surprise party in my honour; officially accrediting my first solo professional brilliance. I was startled to find Mother and Grandpa joining me in my achievements and felicitating me for the job well done. I was too confounded to express my emotions. But then sometimes it's alright to let life endorse you, especially when it has inflicted you with unspeakable agonies. When I finally couldn't decide how to react to life's unexpected treatment with me, I hugged Ma and Grandpa and said in a suppressed voice…

"I wish he'd have been alive to see this special day of his daughter's life."

The party lasted for almost the entire day, and I was overwhelmed to see the full strength of "Ignis" along with their families, stealing time from their busy lives to sort of commemorate my endeavours and encourage me to keep marching. As we all were about to wrap up and leave, we heard a commanding voice attracting everyone's attention. It was Siddhartha.

"Ladies and Gentlemen. Before these rare moments fade and we all leave to the promises of tomorrow, I'd like to say a few words in honour of our youngest member and every person associated with this organisation. It's one of those rare days when we gather and revere in unison. I recall when Mrs. Sikand proposed her name to me for something that never occurred in the history of this organisation, a "Sabbatical." Honestly, I wasn't too certain about inducting her. But then she briefed me about her in detail, she narrated me tales of her imperishable zeal to seek and carve her own path for truth, something that no one else can grant us but our own honest endeavours. And that has been the very core belief of this venture. When I started up with "Ignis," I dreamed of having people like you on my side, working along passionately for the sake of contributing towards that ideal society which we all often shrug off as something too "elusive to achieve" in times like these and today when I see you guys giving their best for the common goal, I believe I didn't fail."

There was a thunderous applause in response to his commendable speech. Yet, in moments like these, when success suddenly shoots to your head, when the future seems too promising, when you fail to recognise the true worth of your work and start juxtaposing the ever-inscrutable roles, in such blank moments, people often do something that unintentionally reveals a not so perfect picture of an apparent design.

Everybody went dead silent when Ayesha's undulating voice furrowed up the otherwise perfect decorum of the evening. "This may be a party spoiler to you, Siddhartha, but I am sure this young lady here bears the talent and she deserves a chance to be involved in that quest to seek out real solutions to those unsolved conundrums lying unattended in the Archives for years. I am particularly pointing at your unclosed ones." There was a grave silence upon his face but collecting his composure back, he replied gently to her and, in a sense, to all of us.

"I think we all have certain issues in our lives that no one else can do much about. Speaking about them, I believe sometimes we ourselves fail to calculate when the time is ripe for them to be attended and dealt with finally. No one else can possibly know the same despite their true and honest intentions, let alone be a part of their real or imaginary solutions. Yet, I am too glad that you keep such high hopes for her, Ayesha. In fact, we all share the same fervour for her, and I promise I won't shy away from taking any person's help to those "unattended ones" at the right moment…"

Rachna took the initiative in taking Ayesha out of the party, who was imbibing too much and was unable to perceive the things happening around caused by her own stirrings.

The party overall ended on a positive note with some heartfelt performances from kids and spouses of faculty members. In the fading moments of the evening, I saw certain incomprehensible bouts of trauma on Mr. Pathak's face, but I preferred refraining myself from countering him in such a vulnerable situation.

The next day it was "business as usual" for everyone, even for Ayesha, who was working in a very composed manner like any normal day. I initially surmised that she'd be oblivious to yesterday's happenings and no one might have discussed with her, which was a sane thing too. Yet she, albeit haphazardly, had initiated something that caught my curiosity earlier also, and this time, I didn't want to let it slip again. So, I decided to ask her in detail about the same, hoping against hope that she might reveal something truly valuable to me this time around.

"Hi Ayesha. Hope you are feeling better now."

"Of course, I am fine. What possibly could have happened to me, by the way?"

"I was concerned about yesterday's incident. You were on the booze and said something which might have offended Siddhartha. But you might not be aware so…"

"Did I mention something about Archives? Gosh, I did it again.."

"So you do that often?"

"Siddhartha never fails to hail the achievements of any young scholar who joins his organisation. Things have been pretty much the same for some time now. They come, learn the intricacies of work and leave for the green pastures out there; leaving him all alone, as if... I am not ashamed of it but yes it's true that I can't keep that much patience. So I don't shy away from speaking out my mind on such occasions when I am sure, that the person of interest here would be leaving him sooner or later for his own self-interest."

"I don't see any sense in keeping such grudges for people about leaving or staying Ayesha. It's their independent will to pursue or leave which none can alter or try to influence even. And regarding proffering any help, do you really think he wants to come out of his own hermetic world of self-inflictions?"

"No. No. No! There never have been self-inflictions Sara. Don't mistake him for being a masochist for God's sake! He never was, not even for a single moment. It was his vision to have a section like archives in the organisation. He was the one who inspired all of us here when we almost gave up on our inscrutable researches, when we failed to come up with something, even erroneous. Through his strong conviction, the team got inspired to tread that extra mile for the truth and with time, they became convinced and profoundly involved. The archives noticed a paradigm shift from the unsolved cases to the solved ones. He dreamed that one day this section would become world-famous for its reference real case studies. But ironically, the man who guided people in seeking answers was left alone for his own unsolved ones. You'd be surprised, Sara, that all the archive cases have been solved and made opened as reference case studies which anyone can access anytime; barring his own inexplicable ones that are still in the dark awaiting a justifiable closure."

"With such brilliant faculty around, it seems rather implausible to me that a certain rational conclusion couldn't be reckoned for those unsolved ones."

"It isn't that faculties were never helpful. There have been numerous files in the references that detail their contributions in resolving his twisted ones too. Yet as per my records, there are still two cases pending and those have not been touched for long. It seems either he isn't getting time from his busy schedule or he has lost all hopes of a possible unravelling. But whatever it may be, I wish there could be an early resolution to these as I've seen him secretly attending to those cases and tormenting himself for hours in that lonely quest..."

In a jiffy, I read his solved files from references. Indeed, they were profound, an erudite source of psychology and its pure application. These are classic examples of making the turgid psychological approaches more comprehensively effective for a layman. They exhibited fine methods of alleviating the sufferings of people through rational psychological approaches and remarkably intuitive techniques, which were so far very rarely applied, let alone known in common practice.

As I read them in-depth and acknowledged the painstaking efforts involved in their elucidation, I felt a sudden pang in my heart for being an active part of such complexities. Ayesha told me that when these archives were made public, there was an uproar, especially among the educated masses, that every now and then, scholars from world-renowned universities and other academic institutions started chasing Siddhartha and other team members desperately. While many were bent on the lucrative proposals, he never did. It was an eye-opener moment for me as well, for whatever I learned from my professional studies or inherited through my intuitive skills, I could never have imagined discerning such a fine milieu of their applications.

Be it the impact of the impeccable research or my unbridled urge to be a part of seeking the truth of the final unresolved ones, nothing in the whole damn world seemed more elusive to me than the quest for the answers that were tantalizingly lurking and ripping my mind off in the foliage of their dense curiosity. Suddenly, I was clear about my priority for the remaining tenure of the sabbatical. I wanted to endure such extremities to hone myself for better learning and a bright prospect of excelling in this complex field.

I decided to confront him, as he was the only one holding the final images in his mind whilst others were only keeping the pieces of an unsolved jigsaw! I was only waiting for that opportune moment to segue myself into those treacherous realms of psychology, which, albeit I was aware of, I had never been able to apply myself to such live applications. Siddhartha was in the office for a few days to develop action plans for future projects. I deliberately planned to refrain from field operations till some time for obvious reasons! It was a foggy January morning, and I was already late.

As I reached there, jostling, I found him standing frozen in the archives. The chilling wind flowing inside through the carelessly opened windows further fortified the already reticent ambience pervading over. The levitating fog ambitiously tried to engulf the whole section along with the person who started this all. There was an undecipherable countenance on his face while he was engrossed in one of the files. It was hard for me to assume who was more loyal to him in those moments- his memories, which were, after all, memories, destined to fade and wither away with receding time or that chilling wind with fog as her accomplice toiling hard in silence to console him, conjuring him for burying that past inside him eternally, for the world does not deserve such pious crusades.

Amid that playa of his own tribulations, it was me-watching him. Keeping no emotions of sympathy or pain. Callous, I may be, as my heart was now conditioned not to be a part of anyone's painful quest. I often treated myself partially with despise and acquiesce for bearing such rude behaviour. Yet it was an exception, as I wanted to be a part of his quest out of my own eccentricity and was not shying away from being his helping hand in resolving the mysteries of his life... While shutting the windows, I spoke to him in a jest.

"You might be finding your feet in these chilly surroundings, but frankly, I felt freezing in here."

He shuddered a bit only to realise the slightly intruding presence of someone else in his "Personal time".

"Oh. I am sorry I didn't notice the open windows. I must confess I have feelings for the cool winter breeze falling upon my face. This soothing whiff of mist never ceases to bring the eventful memories of my glorious childhood days when we used to play soccer in the lush green meadows of the Shimla countryside. It was a brief stint for the family due to business exigencies but certainly a remarkable experience for us in its entirety. Anyways, how are the projects going on?"

"Well, they are fine, very fine indeed. I realised I never expressed my gratitude to you personally for giving a neophyte mind like me a worthy platform to enrich and learn."

"Not to forget, Madam Sikand. It was her efforts in the beginning."

"Of course. I am not shy to admit that I could never have acquired such brilliant professional experience elsewhere, and her role in all this is indelible."

"I am happy too Sara. It's always gratifying to see young, ardent minds shaping themselves willfully to serve."

"Yes, but sometimes serving alone is not enough. You must learn to take that firm stand against your inflictions, too. After all, you can serve perfectly well only when you have learned to make peace with yourself."

"Peace and perfection are often deceiving. It takes time to learn when they're egotistical or symbiotic."

"I am not scared to be deceived. I am sure, unlike humans, these won't leave such lasting scars upon my existence."

"Sara, I think you have taken your life too seriously. Don't smother it by shaping it into a turgid prose... let yourself flow. It's not the time to brood so vehemently over the scars and all. I agree it's a serious business, but you need not always feel the weight on your shoulders. Learn to live and enjoy your life to its optimum. It's great that you keep a dream in life and pain somehow propels it, yet use it as a catalyst rather than a stalwart associate."

"I am not a masochist, in case you are mistaken to believe me. In fact, if I am not wrong, there are people around who prefer themselves to be hermetically sealed in certain archive sections as if they succumbed to their own stubbornness or perhaps a timid will of which others are unworthy or too feeble to be involved..."

"That's absolutely untrue, Sara. Archives never operated that way here. I am not running a sleuth business, for God's Sake. There always have been people around who were part of the solutions, and through their courage and diligence alone, this section has attained what it's truly worthy of."

"For that truth alone, I am standing here brazen! You have every right to dismiss me for intruding, yet I'd keep trying to be a part... Why hide away Mr Pathak and till when? Why run away from those unsolved files?"

"I am not hiding anything and neither running from something. As I told you earlier, there have always been people who were aware of these cases, and they tried, too. I know your intrusion is for the sake of learning alone, and it can never be audacious, but ironically, no one can do much to assuage the intensity which they bear. Nothing personal, Sara. But isn't it true that some wars are meant to be fought alone?'

"Before being a part of "Ignis", I kept somewhat similar notions. But whatever I inherited here, I can affirm to you that sometimes people deserve a chance to be a part of your war. But in my case, as you deduced astutely, I won't be offering you any moral support as I know you have transcended the support of analgesics in life. It's my request to work alongside you for my professional enrichment alone. That's my sole interest, and I think I deserve a fair chance based on my progress so far."

His probing eyes stared deep into mine as if he was trying to sieve my soul for a purpose. At last, he broke his dominating, uncomfortable silence.

"You are brave, but sometimes bravery alone will not suffice. If you can assure me that you deserve a fair chance, then I can assure you that once you are a part, you'd never be able to part yourself; either by force or by choice, you won't succeed. You have a day's time to reconsider… Tomorrow, I'd be leaving to wage my final stand against the first conundrum. If your mind still wishes to be involved, I'd be leaving Delhi at 09.00 a.m. sharp."

That entire night, I deliberated about his admonishment and my will to be involved. Sometimes, I inferred him as a timeless traveller treading upon the same path again and again, which was a repercussion of his own stale choices. As a result, it felt to me as if a Puritan streak had etched itself so deeply into a certain niche of his mind that his perception towards sufferings was that of reverence, and his toiling was dedicated to ennobling their strength. I was firm more than ever now to be a part of his endless labyrinths for my own selfishness, leading only to better prospects of learning and gaining professional acumen.

It was a foggy Sunday morning, and I was ready with all the baggage I could possibly afford and anticipate for the journey ahead. I was waiting for him on the same lawn that once had smitten me to that trance-like state. Now, I could barely appreciate the magnificent beauty of the same. The mist-shrouded it and was flowing towards me intermittently. I could feel its chill on my face, partially making my mind numb. But then I let it happen and closed my eyes, hoping against hope that my neophyte mind would finally succeed in making certain fissures in the immortal empire of time to have a glimpse of the future. But then, as time might have appeared out of its omnipresence, I felt a sharp focus of light falling upon my eyes, forming a luminous halo of present around my thoughts, which were daring to breach into the territories of an unseen future. I saw him driving towards me. While I was keeping my baggage in the rear, I noticed him gazing meditatively at the same lawn. As I seated myself beside him in the front, I saw a look in his eyes very similar to what the primordial explorers of the Orient might have greeted one another while anticipating the tortuous voyages ahead.

"All set?"

His words reverberated in the mist with the same gusto as they did in my strangely.

Vivacious heart at that moment. I beamed in delight, affirming him to cruise along the thick miasma that was cloaking the horizon of an unseen future.

Chapter Twelve

Our destination was Rampur, one of the prominent districts of Uttar Pradesh. Situated at about 196 kilometers from the National Capital, the city had had a very interesting past. He narrated its history in a nutshell on our way to the city. He said that earlier, it was ruled by "Katheria Rajputs, who fought for over four hundred years with the rulers of Delhi and later with the Mughals. The city then had a reign of Nawabs, who built distinct monuments and buildings signifying the presence of Mughal-type architecture.

Surprisingly, he was a prominent figure in the town. I was astonished to receive such benign salutations from so many people in an altogether new place, but then I recalled Siddhartha's yearlong expedition of the country as told by Ayesha, and I framed a logical conclusion to such greetings. For the initial few days, he recommended that I be acquainted with the surroundings, as it would be extremely helpful for future courses of action. He wanted me to do it alone and suggested that I avoid getting any help from any guide. He said, "Exploring a new place is like learning to ride a bicycle; no one can precisely teach you how to make that fine balance with the machine but yourself."

Enduring a glorious past, Rampur certainly had very special places to explore. I commenced my journey with the Koti Khas Bagh. It was actually a palace and an erstwhile residence of the Nawab of Rampur. The sprawling 300-acre compound abided by the huge 200-room European-style palace. The unique blend of Islamic and British architecture evinced the history of the city as a pliant state under British protection until Independence.

The other fascinating features of the palace were the music room and the personal cinema hall of Nawabs. Adorned with the eye-catching "Burma Teak" and "Belgian glass" chandeliers, the huge halls of the palace personified the versatile architecture of a bygone era. The other prominent places of the city which I explored were the Rampur Planetarium, Mohammad Ali Jauhar University, and the Shadab Market surrounding the famous Jama Masjid of Rampur, the foundation of which was laid by Nawab Faizullah Khan, who ruled Rampur from 1774 to 1794. But it was the Raza library that entrusted me with a perfectly ecstatic experience worthy of acquiring a special place in any art lover's heart. Folklore and historians concurred that it was "Nawab Faizullah Khan" who established the library in the last decades of the eighteenth century, initially stocking it with his personal collection of ancient manuscripts and miniature specimens of Islamic calligraphy. The future heirs, too, were great patrons of art, music and literature, and the library grew by giant strides.

Being one of the biggest libraries of Asia, it inherited printed works in other important languages also like Sanskrit, Hindi, Pashto, Urdu, Turkish and Tamil. An estimated 30,000 printed books in various other languages were a part of its immortal legacy.

With time, I was on my way in achieving that fine, elusive balance with the new place, as recommended by him. Meanwhile, he was busy in his own preoccupations and we seldom met during that first week of our halt. I was too keen now to unveil the purpose of our visit until finally we got a chance to meet and have our dinner together. I knew the time was now to ferret out the aim of this seemingly obscure sojourn.

"I am very much impressed by the historical monuments and the fascinating history of this remarkable place."

"Hmmm... Indeed. You must have visited the Koti Khas Bagh and the mesmerising Raza library. It's really very hard to pull yourself off their legacies. For anyone, it won't be tough to associate some part of oneself to these great monuments."

"Must be having certain remarkable memories for this place then, isn't it?"

Our eyes met, and he sort of evaded my straight glance until, finally, he left the dinner table and stood motionless in front of the balcony window. His hands gently wiped the mist off the windowpane as if he was trying to arouse the frozen past of an impassive town while seeking the courage to revive his own as well. The mist mildly cascaded upon the glass that was acting more or less like an interface between the intersection of two enduring pasts, desperately waiting for its fate to shatter and let them merge as one... Never before had I felt such power in a patient's heart until that very moment. I was about to leave when his voice echoed in the dark. It was my turn now to withstand those pasts which had finally chosen to merge as one. I could feel the mysteriously silent darkness with its thousand images inscribed in the smithereens of that levitating interface, which finally met with its fate conspiring with those screeching pasts, cruising towards me with undecipherable intentions. I closed my eyes to brace myself.

'It was the fall of 2005, and I was on a mission to delve as far as I could into the psyche of industrial labour. On my restive tread, I changed many profiles and traversed almost the entire Nation. It was my deliberate planning to work along the most obdurate of the unions of the country to extract clarity in my purpose. My research led me to be a part of many such ordeals like the one I endured here.

There used to be a steel mill located somewhere in the rural suburbs of this city where I was appointed as chief of "Industrial Relations", and my job was to ensure cordial working relations with the Union and the Management. Since the trade union over there was famous for its strikes and creating unrest over trivial issues, my primary job was to avert, as far as I could, the incidents leading to such clashes. My tenure over there was hailed as the most peaceful one in the history of the mill since its inception. I toiled hard to ensure the unison rise of both ends. But as they say, every good thing finally comes to an end. My reign, too, was once challenged by severe industrial unrest, leading to periods of intermittent strikes over the issue of bonuses. Their demands were too illogical and detrimental to the very future of the mill, which clearly indicated an inkling of certain external influences smeared with the hideous intentions of the corrupt insiders. Of course, I was firm on my decision to get it negotiated on common grounds as I was aware of the management's intentions to shift the mill to an altogether new location, and that could only have meant a bleak, dark future for thousands of labourers along with their families. But then, apart from me, there were many others who were genuinely concerned about the future of the local people. One such person was in my department whose efforts were more pious and serious than mine. She was on my team and was famous in the mill for seeking out breakthroughs in numerous such strikes.

Shraddha Pandey, aka "Mangal Pandey", as they fondly named her. She was one rebel of a person. Her tough and determined character conferred her with many laurels from management and labour unions alike. She was, by all means, the undisputed successor of my designation in the company, and frankly, I was molding her too for that position. But then, the path to glory can never be complete without inheriting true enemies. On one of the most agitated of days, somebody attacked her with acid, causing permanent disfigurement of her face. The same day, I was at the labour commissioner's office working out a way to concur with him and the labour union officials. We were on the verge of resolving that gruesome strike when this terrible incident occurred. In the wake of the situation being exacerbated, the management took the overnight decision of a permanent shutdown, and since then, the mill has never been operational. Her case was callously attended by the authorities. I could never forget the look in her parent's eyes when they pilloried me, blaming me for her predicaments. But of all the inflictions, I could never forgive myself for the fact that to date, I could not do anything for that brave soul, who sought nothing but a secure future for her people.'

'But what could you possibly do to avert the attack? I don't approve of you being blamed for all this. Yet I am concerned that you could not do anything for her.'

'Yes, to any outsider, I am never to be blamed. But no matter what, I cannot evade myself from the truth that people, in those moments, in that simmering cauldron of rage and the quest for a hypothetical crusade of equality, were having their most opportune moments to settle old scores, and they eventually did.

You know, Sara, I anticipated the attack on her on that fateful day but could not have imagined it to be so brutal. Had she been with me during those decisive moments, things could have been different for her and probably for the mill too; yet I chose to leave her there, upon the vent of an erupting volcano, because I wanted her to learn and inherit as much as she could from such situations. It was a risk I took for her better, and I could never forgive myself for taking it… I still remember her lying in that cold hospital ward, left to suffer in her own destitute. I could not refrain myself from telling her the truth about myself. She was impassive when she heard about my real intentions of joining the firm and refused my proposal of bearing all the costs of her plastic surgery. It was all over for me, but then she gave me one chance to redeem myself. Her only condition was that she would earn the requisite money and would never accept any philanthropy from my end."

"So what have you planned now?"

"Kite flying is one of the most cherished sports in this region of the state. People bet hefty amounts in the competition. I have decided to bet ten lakhs in the upcoming weekend competition, which is precisely the estimated cost of her surgery from the most renowned medical institute. Shraddha is going to be my partner. She will have to be. Brace yourself, Sara. The storm is staring deep into our eyes, and this silence is only a mirage…"

In the wake of such hefty prize money being finalised, the organisers did their best to disseminate the information as far as they possibly could, with clear intentions of making the event as grand as possible. For the days before the anointed day, the city witnessed the flocks of eager enthusiasts and adept professionals jostling with each other to get their fair chance to participate in one gala of an event. Through innumerable preliminaries for making the competition turn to its true expectations, fifty-odd participants were finalised for the final duel. Siddhartha, the organisers, and I witnessed all those prelims.

I was enthralled by the sheer intensity of the competition, and honestly, with such master crafters of the flying solo, I feared a very bleak chance of his redemption. And then, finally, he showed me the battleground chosen for the final face-off. It was a big, bereaved ground, drowsily stretched out in the outskirts of the town, misled of its inefficacy by the disdain of the glances, or maybe living with its own choice of being untamed, yet ironically being chosen for its destined purpose to overt a fight for justice in not such a just world of which it was an inseparable part! While he was ruminating over certain concerning things in his mind, I tried to insinuate myself to be of help in the final face-off. When the only decipherable noise amongst us was of the frosty, blowing wind and complaining thicket, I decided to intervene.

"So, does she know that you're here? About all of this?"

"Can't say yet, but I am sure some past acquaintance would have informed her."

"Do you believe she'd come to this? Pardon me, I don't wish to malice your efforts, but people change with time…"

"Of course, they do! But sometimes you deserve to fight against time… I know where she is in the city, and tomorrow, I'll be facing her after all these years. To convince her amid the objections of all the time that passed silently between us since then! I planned to go alone earlier, but you can join me if you wish to."

"I will come with you!"

And then both of us marched together, away from that wasteland, until I noticed a spire-like pattern rose against the gloomy thicket and an overcast sky. Before I could utter a word, I saw Siddhartha's mien. It was hard to believe for me, but he could squirm at any moment! But then he gasped for some chill from the frost around to harden his heart and spake.

"Still standing like an agonising mistake of a vindictive past. Never failing to raise its head in the most vulnerable of times. Sara, that used to be the steel mill where this all started."

Moving silently through those dank, dark streets of an otherwise throbbing city, we finally managed to reach the house of Shraddha Pandey. Hesitatingly, he knocked on the door and instantly stepped back as if the door was infected by the same vindictive past that had devoured him ever since he came back to make peace with it!

I heard a slow, harmonious gait echoing against the silence of the ambience. The door was finally opened for us, and we were greeted by that dismal yet serene persona. When that calm gaze fell upon him, I sensed a sudden surge of emotions waiting to be exhaled at any moment- if only a person could seek respite from cruel misunderstandings; but then the words were buried inside when a voice reverberated through that bleak, frigid, windswept home.

"Who's that Baba?"

Tears trickled down from Siddhartha's eyes as he stood there frozen, begging that serene one, who was now impassive to his emotions, to let him in. And then I saw a faint image cloaked in black, with a partially covered face rising against the crumbling walls.

Her unwavering gaze was fixed upon his eyes with no element of awe or happiness inscribed, a kind of gaze that can deride the very existence of any sane life, and not all can keep them from shattering, but it was him; the only one I ever encountered, to question life on its esoteric meander!

"What do you wish to seek now from us after so many years? Can you even imagine what our lives have been all through? Her mother couldn't bear all this and died. Nothing but aimless nomads, that's what we have been ever since."

"Uncle, I accept that I am very much to blame for your irrevocable losses. I should have saved her that day, but… I searched for her everywhere but in vain! And now that I've finally got a chance to amend things, wouldn't you give me the fair chance that I deserve?"

"What can you do for us now?"

And then he disclosed his whole plan and his intentions of involving her as his partner on that fateful day.

“Have you gone insane? Do you wish to get us outcast from here? Can you even imagine how much we have endured for this morsel of a livelihood, and you wish to snatch that too from us? Consider the notions of society. They'd make it impossible for us to survive here. How does it matter to you? Win or lose! You'd desert us like you did so many years ago. I am too old and feeble to face it all over again now, son! For God's sake, leave us to our own fate.”

‘But uncle...’

‘No, son! Not again, for God's sake!’

And he started pushing us vehemently out of the door but then, like a silver lining in the clouds, like a truth itself to an altogether counterfeit life, she finally broke her silence.

‘Shraddha will rise, Sir! She will rise, Father. For her rights, for herself, she will rise.’

‘Are you out of your mind? What about society?’

‘Which society, Baba? Where were all those people when we were inflecting alone? Whatever we have achieved today since that day, we did it with our unflinching will not to give up, and you know that, Baba! No one is accredited to be with us in our darkest hour but ourselves! I am amazed that there are still people like him who know life so closely, and I'd sacrilege all my inheritance if I stepped back now... I'd definitely give that chance to your vision, Sir! Win or lose matters least to me now, but I feel that if I stood for this war, I'd be able to face millions of others to come...'

And so we left the place with a hope of finally amending the things. I could feel a certain positive energy being enthused in him for the very first time since our sojourn. In haste, he spoke. "You've been nothing less than a lucky charm, Sara! I hope the lady luck will smile upon me on that final face, too," For the rest of the day, he learned about the intricacies of the magnificent sport from the masters of the craft. It was an enchanting view to see people from almost a bygone era being resurrected by choice and helping a man seek his redemption, and none amongst them had any slightest idea about it. Interestingly, this man was from an era that was as callous to them as they were to it, but then humanity never hinged upon the sanguinity of temperaments; it only sought a noble cause worth endeavouring for, which fortunately he had!

Although, I was never a part of the whole mess and there was nothing I could do to mend it, yet I felt myself as an integral part of whatever pious was happening around. In those moments, I reminisced his admonish and realised that he was right, I'd never be able to part myself from these intensely complex cases either by choice or by will!

He chose to fly a yellow kite. The above of the same was concave rather than the usual convex. The designer gave it the eye of an eagle, and on its tail, the feather of a lark was etched, making it appear like a fierce bird of prey waiting to be unleashed! In that dim shaft of sunset, which was piercing the heart of that wonderful creation, I saw something, some kind of short note written. It was Siddhartha's writing. I held it firm to decipher that sort of encryption against the background of those receding shafts of light, and it made sense as I read… "Hush the clamour of real. Let me delve into the straits of my foolish unreal… who cares for those receding, mocking voices? Once again, let me hold a hand. Ain't I, after all this, worthy of what the learned call a yearned sleep?"

A sudden gush of air unfurled it from my grip. I knew I was too enervating, by all my efforts and inheritance, to hold something sacred like that for so long.

With the first ray of light from the heavens above, the city started witnessing an unprecedented flock of noisy tourists and natives alike, throbbing, jostling towards the destination, which was the arena for many and a pilgrimage for a few. I suited myself to the traditional attire and noticed a sudden warmth of acceptance emanating from the mass's gestures and behaviour, as if culture was like a modicum of that catalyst that ignited humanity in people's hearts. Smitten by that cacophony of delirium, I felt myself trapped and very much a part of that seemingly exciting tale, which made me realise ecstatically that being a part of this venture was probably one of the best decisions of my life.

Being a part of the organising committee and the highest bidder of the prize money, Siddhartha was by default exempted from the preliminaries and had to compete with the final ten kite flyers that were expected to be the best of the best.

I could see him looking cogitatively at his fellow kite flyers with their kites soaring in the endless blue. There was no fear of failure in his eyes, yet there was a yearning for someone's arrival. By the next few hours, the competition finally acquired its final ten flyers. As expected and known, they were the best the competition could probably offer, enriched and rooted with skill and experience. They, indeed, were resolute, astute flyers with an iron will to steal the glory gleaming in their triumphant eyes.

There was an announcement made for the rest of an hour before that final confrontation, and still, there was no sign of Shraddha. He looked at me with wearing inquisitiveness in his eyes. I wish I could provide him more than a spurious persistence frailly portrayed in the fraudulent canvas of my eyes. But then he deciphered it instantly and smiled generously, making it impossible for me to construe if he had forgiven me or blamed himself instead! The hour passed like an insubstantial array of time's motifs when, finally, the announcement was made for the final contenders to gather with their kites and partners. I saw him picking up his kite and the kite string roller and walking with a shambolic gait towards the field until he stood frozen with his gaze fixed upon the horizon. I saw a black, velvet-like image arising out of the pristine fog, which had already begun to levitate with the preceding day. I saw a thousand moments of triumph in those coruscating cascades from his eyes. It was her flowing towards him like a symphony of past which bowed to him and finally drifted his stance of being vindictive to forgiving!

And then they all flew together. Some with a reckless compulsion of victory so vividly conspicuous that one could see a thousand untold tales of an otherwise hackneyed life, tales that were resurrected one after another as mute incantations wishing to sway anyone who dared to behold! Some with a burden of survival were being thrown upon their shoulders, which was suited to embolden them for this once-in-a-lifetime occasion of making that leap of faith.

But who could stop the terror of a tense moment, as hands trembled and a kite flew above, circling as if it mirrored the chaos in their minds, while a critical crowd watched, quick to mock failure? Amid this intense chaos, a noisy mix brewing like a potion of human hopes and struggles, I saw two brave individuals endure silent criticism, facing the spite that was the crowd's only reaction to their efforts. Who could ignore the ultimate power of truth, the final act of regret for a lost purity and redemption; a regret deeper and more bitter than they could have imagined or contained within their numb hearts?

Siddhartha was skilled. His expertise helped him defeat many competitors, leaving only three in the contest. The crowd grew wild as they neared victory. Suddenly, a sharp whistle cut through the calm sky. I was amazed to see eagles flying with the kites, sometimes tangling with them. I learned this was an old competition trick, where participants or even outsiders release these birds to disrupt others. The real challenge was to protect your kite against any obstacle to claim victory. These eagles were trained for just such disruptions, a final obstacle looming over someone's dream of winning, driving them to take desperate actions without any concern from the crowd. There's nothing more upsetting to the public than seeing the usual upset by the underdogs.

Meanwhile, the duel was left between the final two challengers, when one of the eagles, on the command of certain, shrilling sound left snapping the kite and flew ferociously towards Shraddha, pouncing upon her face as if she was a vulnerable prey. The cloak shrouding her charred face was torn asunder for the world to see its irrevocable failure, a virulent wound capable of devouring a whole civilisation in its shame!

Siddhartha's voice choked for her name in desperation, but then her voice froze rather than awakened the souls of the masses as she said, "No, Sir! Let me ascend today myself; if I don't step up here, I'll never advance again, anywhere" There was an appalling silence in the crowd and then everybody protested violently against the heinous act! Immediately, the sky was cleared of the unwanted, and his final act of mastery snipped the final one, banishing its all further guises in the face of the firmament.

There was a thunderous applause in the crowd. I couldn't believe my eyes when I saw them shouting, *"Yeh uski Marzi hai, Yehi uski Marzi hai..."* (This is his will, this alone is his will). I saw Siddhartha falling down to his knees with his hands firmly clasping his face and his torso undulating in extreme emotions. Shraddha was standing by her side, accepting all the accolades of the society, who was finally convinced and acknowledged her brutal struggle. There was a standing ovation in the crowd for this extraordinary fleet of human endeavour.

With glinted eyes, I saw the sun shining brightly upon the same spire, the last contemporary ruin of the Steel mill. That had once intimidated him was now like an epitome of persistence rising to the occasion. The crowd was still clapping, cheering, and dancing to their glory with their loud, deep, mellifluous shibboleth *"Yeh uski Marzi hai, Yehi uski Marzi hai..."* (This is his will, this alone is his will).

Chapter Thirteen

My notion of Siddhartha bearing a firm temperament for Shraddha soon got repealed as he never insisted her once to reconsider her pursuits of achieving higher education for the sake of joining him at the IGNIS.

While we were on our way back to New Delhi from that unforgettable sojourn, I was in a dilemma as to how one could finally bid adieu to such a person without even asking once for mulling over the decisions; there always remains an integral bond with a person who had been a part of someone's perpetual reckoning for almost a decade! Amid the warmth of a wintry sunny afternoon and lush green surroundings, we were travelling as if a silent yet firm command of time towards the unforeseen ventures lurking ahead. In that utterly discreet silence, he succeeded in reading my thoughts, and whatever ensued will always be etched in my mind, which was still gasping to cull a plausible sense out of whatever happened in the past few days.

"I know you might be having mixed reactions over my decision of letting her go forever again from our lives, there's hardly an iota of doubt as how invaluable asset she was for the IGNIS and its ventures and what laurels she could bring for herself and the organisation, yet there are certain decisions which don't demand interventions; Sometimes you need to lose the most precious for the sake of it..."

I could see a rare glint from the corner of his eye. Realising I caught him in his act, he abruptly opened the window of the car and a fine breeze shrouded that tearful abode for her in his eyes. In those rare moments I saw a blend of patience, sacrifice and bravery dancing merrily in his eyes. Who says heroes are destined to be impassive marionettes for the sake of their fateful burdens!

With its creepy-crawly pace, life webbed us all in its intricacies and soon the organisation was pushed to its limits when the projects poured in from literally all spheres of the human domain keeping us all on our toes and saturating every single one of us to such an extent that by the end of the year all of us were craving for a worthy break.

Like all good things eventually come to their expected ends, I, too, was on the verge of completing my stint with the amazing organisation. I wasn't feeling too sentimental about the end of my Sabbatical, but there was certainly an ache inside for losing such a phenomenal run through which I inherited more than I paid back, causing an ache inside that I'd always be indebted to this wonderful venture throughout my life and will strive to be there on the first call if my services were called for in the future. With my remaining days, I contemplated more about my decision to continue with my master's and occasionally thought about that final unresolved mystery breathing surreptitiously in the archives. With every passing day, I could feel that uncomfortable wheeze upon my neck proliferating and teasing with a feeling that it was this now or never moment to unravel the truth and like always, I started waiting for that one opportune moment to pounce upon and grasp it…

Siddhartha was, as usual, too preoccupied with his new projects, and without his consent, Ayesha could never have let me intrude into the Archives for that file. With the little time I was left with, I somehow knew that it wouldn't be possible for me to resolve it along with him as I did with the earlier one, but then I didn't want to leave without at least trying my hand on the conundrum. Just a week before my adieu, he returned to the office, and once again, I started to subterfuge and pounce upon the unfinished business. I could infer from his guileless mien and my professional reasoning that it'd be more ethical and exact to put forward my request very succinctly to him to at least have a look at the case for reference sake, and then finally, I dared to ambush him again…

"Must be very busy indeed with new projects pouring in."

"Yeah, dear, it's been a very busy run. The team is asking for leave, and no one can complain about it. This time of the year should always be spent with family, and they deserve it, too."

"Indeed! I noticed you are working on their behalf. It's pretty unusual to see the CEO doing overtime for an employee's vacation's sake! I wonder you never gave a thought of having your own family too..."

"Oh, why, I have my family Sara! I'd be planning to spend some quality time with them, too."

"Yes, of course! But I think you know what I was hinting towards. As per my sincere advice, you should not delay any further. The time is reckoning you to get married and repose upon this aspect of life too."

"Ha Ha Ha! Oh dear, you sound like my mother! Who'd marry someone who sort of married to his own work?"

"Well, Mr Pathak, don't behave like you're too impervious to such emotions. I've hardly met anyone who's never been into such things, particularly love! You are a flawless one to know human emotions, and people crave such company! It's hard to believe this strong emotion never confronted you, or is it also advised to keep mum in the archives?"

I could see him shuffling the sheets, reporting the latest developments in the newly offered projects, when he stopped and stared deeply into my eyes. The strange smile on his face was too difficult to fathom until, finally, he broke his uncomfortable silence.

"Speaking about love, Sara... It's through treading so often upon such unyielding paths which are now engraved too vividly in the recesses of mind and heart, retaining unspoken tales of those incomplete rendezvous, have I realised that love is a lot like attaining that imaginary balance when you're neither too imposing nor too aloof to the person of interest. The real challenge, however, is to be able to acknowledge correctly that time and place when you've actually attained it, for life is like that cruel mirage that's never going to disclose if you are towards, afar or ironically upon that elusive state..."

"Very well, Mr. Pathak. I never knew you kept such poetic propensities! So how many of the poor creatures have been hanging in that imaginary, elusive balance of your love, by the way?"

"Why, Sara? What's my fault for facing this line of fire from your end, by the way? But jokes apart, if you ask me the truth, those poor creatures could never muster the necessary patience to walk beside me in my times of hardships. They often entered and left my life with no compunction, and fortunately, I never found the time to chase them. After all, beyond a certain time frame, a man should be wise enough to know and sense his loyalties and learn to stick to them ardently till the end of the road. And in my simple life, Sara, those loyalties were never people but paths that led me to touch and transform hundreds of desperate lives and then ultimately metamorphosed me too..."

"You'd certainly be having a very hard time married to the unfortunate one. I reckon people say "that" person is way ahead of his time, in your case I must say you are surely born in the wrong times! You belong to the eras of your beloved Socrates. Who knows, maybe an incarnation of one of his avid disciples, if not himself..."

"Ah, Wonderful! All my contemplations finally bore fruit. But what's bothering you, Miss Vasishta? You can ask me blatantly. I feel smothered when people talk to me in masks, and frankly, I am sort of allergic to the ones, too! Moreover, after coming this far, you deserve to stand forth and speak your mind."

"Fair enough, Sir, even I was feeling a bit unsettled, meandering off my true purpose. Actually, my curiosity is consuming the best of me as I realise that I've come to the end of the road with this otherwise wonderful sabbatical and acknowledge that my inheritance would be truly incomplete if I miss anything I believe I could possibly grasp. I know it's wayward on my part, but I was interested to learn about that final unresolved case of yours. I don't wish to offer you any help now, but just for the sake of knowledge and holding on to that, I know something would be unimaginable."

He closed his eyes for a moment and took deep breaths as if weighing all the options available and then replied in a very confident manner.

"I think I can say this very firmly now that the case has been resolved. To the best of my observations, the victim has recuperated and doesn't need any support."

"Recuperated? You mean to say that the one, whosoever he/she may be, has recuperated itself without any external support? Astonishing!"

"Indeed! People are well capable of doing the impossible, and the victim here has always been a towering figure for other victims and normal ones alike."

"I can say that... But for reference alone, I'd like to have a look at it."

"I'd recommend you not indulge in it. Moreover, I've instructed Ayesha not to make it public until I make it ready for reference, and for that, I'd be requiring her and my time for elaborating the entire case history to her. This may take weeks, even months, but certainly much more time than you have left here. It'd be advisable on my part to focus on your future prospects now!"

"Don't talk like I am already passé for this organisation now. I am still a very active part of it, and I think I am worthy of knowing as much as possible of that final unsolved—Oh, I beg your pardon—'Recuperated itself' riddle!"

"I admire your confidence, but I must warn you of so much reliance on your abilities. Sometimes the most fortified of fortresses get inundated through the rivers flowing merrily in their own backyards!"

"Thanks, Siddhartha, for the caution, but I think I've braved enough floods to face another one, if only it's really that momentous!"

"As you like it. Tomorrow I'd be leaving for Kolkata to attend to a project involving the Missionaries over there. I'd instruct Ayesha to show the relevant documents of the same. But then again, I really feel it's unnecessary on your part. I can only advise but never oppose free will."

"Thanks a lot, Siddhartha. I believe this would be our last meeting for some time to come. I want to express my sincere gratitude towards you and the entire 'Ignis' family for being such a dedicated mentor and for precisely everything I inherited!"

"Don't embarrass us! You were wonderful throughout, and I'd definitely try to be there at your farewell party. Can't promise but seriously wish to be there!"

And then we left together. It was already late in the evening, and he, being a chivalrous and concerned one, drove me home. Throughout the way, he was silent while I was vaguely guessing if my presence or absence really mattered to such an incorruptible soul. As I was treading home, he waited till I knocked and it got answered. It was Mama to greet me. When I looked back, he was already gone. I could not believe when my heart shuddered for a moment. It was too early in life for me to feel the pain for someone too difficult to value, yet unbearable to lose, someone like the colourless water, having no true colour of its own yet capable of inheriting any colour from the one who delves in it!

The next morning as I reached the office, Ayesha greeted me with her familiar mischievous smile, but this time there was no derision in it. I could feel proud of myself for earning this genuine respect from someone like her that abruptly flip-flopped in the realms of sanity-insanity and was a brutal mixture of discreet prevarication.

"I got a message from Mr. Pathak earlier in the morning. He told me to open that safe which keeps that one document which no one has ever seen yet but him. I don't have any grudges against you this time Sara! In fact, I am too happy and proud that at last, someone came who dared to make his already messed up life a little less miserable."

"Oh come on, Ayesha! Don't create melodrama for the sake of it. It's just a woman's infatuation with the unknown, and you better know how bitterly compulsive it is. Frankly, how many times did you try breaking the code of the safe by your own?"

"Ha ha, Sara! You're a thing. Come along; let's see where the rabbit hole ends."

And then we jovially went towards the archives like two kids of the kindergarten, embarking upon the unseen, unknown adventure and extremely excited about the same to unravel it. As she unlocked the particular section where our hidden treasure was waiting for us, I saw a very specialised storage cabinet, a sort of safe carefully designed, like the one dedicated for something extremely precious and usually seen in very high-profile museums. There were certain directions advised to be followed and were engrossed upon the rigid walls of that coffer-looking thing. Moving closely, we found that it was written "Temperature to be kept strictly between 18-20 degrees Celsius and Relative humidity between 45-50 percent." There were other very complex arrangements made for the security which were only adding fuel to our already ignited and ceaseless curiosities! When we were done with all the guidelines and procedures, I heard a faint murmur of Ayesha in the dark, "It seems like a letter… a very old and hence well-preserved one."

"A letter? What kind of letter?"

"I don't know! This man is beyond my imagination. So much fuss over a letter!"

"Let's read it. It might belong to one of his darlings…"

Both of us chuckled mockingly and carefully took that fragile piece of paper, which was otherwise fortified against any possible intrusion, even time there seemed objectionable to intrude. While holding it affectionately like a newborn, we brought that hidden lacuna of a buried time to its worthy deserving light. Both of us were fighting like kids for reading it before one another and at last I surrendered to her tantrums, and to which she felt a sense of mawkish pride.

"Okay, enough! Now read it fast, Ayesha. I can't wait any moment longer."

"Wait a little longer, Miss 'Know all'. There are certain things that deserve to be known at their suitable moments."

"Oh, shut up and be quick!"

"Okay, okay, wait a moment."

As she moved her eyes till the end, her face convoluted into an emotion of inexplicable horror. She could not continue with it anymore, and with trembling hands and a choking voice, she proffered it to me.

"This is peculiar, Sara! This letter is addressed solely to you by some Major Sabyasachi Vashista. Who is he, by the way?"

Of all the miseries that a person endures in his life, the past is probably the most crucifying and vindictive. Throughout life, it never unveils its true colours and intentions. A person may be strengthened or may be dilapidated by the sheer memories of one's own, but it remains still, peering silently at our perspectives while mysteriously calibrating the mettle of our soul through its own undecipherable standards, and when it wills, it comes to us; holding our hands through its chilling, unflinching grip, too formidable for anyone to set free from its excruciating clutches.

By the time it clasped me by its tenacious ones, I felt summoned upon by its callous will against which I could not make any objections, let alone thinking of a possible revolt! With a quivering tone and practically in a state of no authority over myself, I replied.

"He was a proud martyr of the Kargil war and the father of an unfortunate girl standing before you at this very moment."

The letter fell from my hands and drifted along silently in that dark, numb alley, wafting away from me like it had been destined forever to. It made no noise as it drifted along. I was astonished to see how analogous the events could turn out to be. He left me as noiselessly as his only living and very much breathing memory was parting from me. I felt a sudden urge of having an absolute volition, with the intervention of absolutely no possible entity. With force, I dragged myself and snatched it with vehemence from whatever unseen force was colluding to part it from me. My heart throbbed and cursed me to put it under such strenuous circumstances yet I held that tiny morsel of my inscrutably, entwined destiny and read it aloud to myself…

Dearest Sara,

This is probably my last communication to you, and only Almighty God knows when the time will be ripe for you to have and cherish it, since I know how much you love me... Pardon me for being so harsh to you, but here lying upon my deathbed and calculating precisely the fading moments of my final hours, I believe this is the only option fate has left me with—to be fierce with my most endearing, the love of my life, and that's you, my dear.

Do you remember the day when you saw me mumbling in the dark and you were scared, left quietly to your bed, believing that I was too stern for my duties and was preparing myself mentally for that looming, imminent war? In reality, I was suffering from a bout of chronic Bipolar II disorder and had opted to bury it within as I could not afford to quit the war due to this godforsaken ailment. My condition worsened during the woeful incidents of the battleground, and the authorities ordered me to leave the war for the safety of myself and my men. I shared the entire trauma with your grandpa in Delhi, and he assured to help me out as he knew certain very good psychiatrists who could help me cope up with this anomaly.

Within a week's time, I got his call, and he was too excited to inform me that with the help of Mrs. Sikand, the Head of Department of Psychology in a leading institute, they finally found someone brave, a young psychologist who was willing to help me out. His name was Siddhartha Pathak, and he was pursuing his education in psychology from abroad and was on a research tour in India. It was too difficult for me to comprehend as to what exactly motivated him to risk his life in such frigid war zones and afflict such pain for a stranger. He was like my shadow for almost all the time and was granted special permissions to attend me on and off the duties. There's no shame in admitting on my part that he was the architect of building the lost faith in me which in turn metamorphosed me miraculously into a crusader in those impossible missions.

It's been snowing very severely here today, and I can anticipate the cruel winters waiting for you in times ahead. Those winters will not be seasonal but conditioned to last through wide swathes of your life. I am feeling too remorseful to depart from all of your lives too soon, yet I am taking this promise from the man I trust the most now, this young fellow Siddhartha. I am taking his promise that he'd help you find meaning and strength in life. I know he is under no moral obligations to us, but I believe he'd never refuse a dying father's last will towards his beloved brave daughter…

Yours forever and alive...
Major Sabyasachi Vashista

My life seemed to me like a jigsaw puzzle, and I silently wondered how every piece of it was put at its correct place from time to time. I suddenly felt an enormous emotional debt upon my soul which could never possibly be redeemed. Baffled by these unprecedented events, I felt myself torn asunder while anticipating the ambiguity of my questionable future. I didn't wait a moment longer there and made up my mind to leave for Kolkata.

While walking alone through those cramped lanes, I was in the realm of a listless yet intermittent contemplation which sunk my heart every time as it reminisced me of that completed jigsaw puzzle whose sense was too grueling for me to accept and inculcate. Nevertheless, I was walking numb with a sense of hope, to the only one I believed, could provide me with something reliable to hold on to in this sheer mayhem.

I found him deeply involved in a conversation with one of the senior most of the missionary nuns, mother superior of the school may be, when our eyes met. I stood there frozen, unable to think of anywhere to recede away, and he sensed it, like he always did. He walked to me in a seemingly discreet gait. Before I could speak, he interjected.

"Your father was one of the bravest persons I ever met in my life. It was clinically impossible for anybody to persist one such moment in a condition like he was in. I was only like a morphine to the pain, sedation to a perpetual adversity. Those mutilated and amputated bodies of soldiers were like a ceaseless fusillade on his deteriorating condition; but he never stepped back an inch from his duty only for your love, Sara! He was your hero and he could never let himself see failing in your eyes. Look at the irony of this life, when we finally tend to decipher the actions of someone like your father, it eclipses the esoteric through the ambiguity of the future."

"You knew! All those years... if you'd have tried, he'd have been alive. You could have convinced him to pull out of the war. I know you could somehow persuade him."

"That is an unbearable truth, Sara! I could have, if I would have. But that was not at all the will of your father. If I somehow could have done that, he'd have been nothing but a marionette of his own remorse and disgust. Tell me, could you have accepted him like that?"

"What about me? What about my whole family? He never gave a thought of our lives without him. Was glory so important that it superseded everything else?"

"It was never about glory, Sara! It was always about things that remain adhered to you conscientiously, throughout your existence. Emanating that force which not only influences the person but many others associated… Both of us could see and feel them in each other's eyes. So, he never wished to be ceased and I never forced him to."

And then suddenly it started raining very hard. In his glinted eyes, I saw the shadow of my father shimmering as if he got reincarnated for a moment and came to me to reveal that in those times, none could be blamed for whatever events that followed in our lives. He ceased to look and left me alone there to accept and form whatever shape I could mold out of the repercussions of their mutual consent. In those falling drops of grace from the firmament that often pretends to be insensitive towards our lives, I heard and deciphered the sense out of destiny's motif. I could see him holding my father innumerable times and witnessing his strength and pain alike, something that none of us could feel or imagine ever again in our lives. I could see him inflicting silently those mute tribulations for keeping that accord for every one of us in the family, if only we could sense it, and I could see him suffering yet walking alone for it till this very day...

And then I ran, piercing the music of destiny, least bothered for the demeanour of the firmament; I ran towards the one none could fathom yet was worth taking a dive for all the sacrifices he had made patiently for us! I ran recklessly against the stubborn will of time and held his hand…

"Please don't leave me now! I don't see any sense in life walking without you in this feckless maze."

They say it's impossible to discern tears in the rain, but the honest ones can never be veiled no matter how intense the deluge is, for they will never hide their true glory like stars shining amid the patches of malevolent clouds.

"You know, Sara, when your father gave me this letter with a promise of making the revelation only when the right time will come, I always believed that I'd never be able to seek that right moment. Out of my own feebleness for making the right judgement, I requested him to not burden me with such gruesome responsibility for I'd never succeed in recognising that moment out of the millions dying every day! He smiled and replied to me calmly, and those were his last words..."

"What did he say?"

He took a deep breath, closing his eyes, reminiscing the heart-wrenching yet probably one of the most cherished moments of his tortuous life, and thus he finally said.

"He said, 'You must not fret Siddhartha. Time will come to you with that moment and you'd never have to seek it. Isn't it true that "*Love is a solitary runner*" capable of empowering us for the impossible? She is my daughter and if her love can make me triumph these cruel, barren treads inside and outside alike; so will mine do to her.' And then he died in peace."

I could finally feel the peace coming to my soul. A peace that was somehow cloaked in his memories and loss; yet it came back finally when it meant the most. The rain between us was only a prelude…

www.ingramcontent.com/pod-product-compliance
Lightning Source LLC
La Vergne TN
LVHW091052150826
845673LV00002B/554